Leaving Wyoming

Leaving Wyoming

A NOVEL BY
LEO BRENT ROBILLARD

TURNSTONE PRESS

Turnstone Press
Artspace Building
607-100 Arthur Street
Winnipeg, MB
R3B 1H3 Canada
www.TurnstonePress.com

Turnstone Press gratefully acknowledges the assistance of The Canada
Council for the Arts, the Manitoba Arts Council, the Government of
Canada through the Book Publishing Industry Development Program and
the Government of Manitoba through the Department of Culture, Heritage
and Tourism, Arts Branch, for our publishing activities.

Cover design: Doowah Design
Interior design: Sharon Caseburg
Printed and bound in Canada by Friesens for Turnstone Press.

Library and Archives Canada Cataloguing in Publication

Robillard, Leo Brent, 1973-
  Leaving Wyoming / Leo Brent Robillard.

ISBN 0-88801-301-9

  I. Title.

PS8635.O237L42 2004   C813'.6   C2004-905694-8

Turnstone Press is committed to reducing the consumption of old growth
forests in the books we publish. This book is printed on acid-free paper that
is 100% ancient forest free.

For Caroline

Leaving Wyoming

Upon a Pale Horse

THE LAWMAN RIDES INTO THE BELLY OF ANOTHER SLEEPLESS night. He is alone. Around him is the world—is the high prairie stretching out toward the sky, with its brush, its blasted trees, and its fields of wild grass. The coulee stretches through it, and before him, like an open throat, sluicing down the sky. Off in the west, there are mountains sleeping like the still hips of a woman. And although the man cannot see them, their presence is unmistakable. His skin is alive to them.

The rains broke an hour ago and the sky is a clean slate. The moon rises like a tossed coin and wings its way above the man's shoulder. It follows him now, a silent metronome tracking his way into morning. And although he is five hundred miles from the nearest sea, he can also sense the tides as they leave the lonely coast of British Columbia for more exotic shores. Fiji. Tahiti. Papua New Guinea. He is a big man who, tonight, more than any other night in his life, knows too well how small he is.

His hands are locked on the reins of his horse. The animal is slow and tired. It snorts into the chill night air. The man is also tired, and cold. His body is packed into the saddle. His shoulders gather about him like a blanket. His skin is as tight as a sunburn, and a fever brews in his eyes. His mind is a fist.

On his boots, his breeches, and the coattails of his oilskin, there is earth—thick cakes of mud dragged north and west from Montana, Wyoming, and as far south as Texas. His hat is shapeless from the rain that has followed him. He is almost sorry to see it pass. Besides the horse, to which he does not speak, the rain has been his only companion. Bullfrogs cry in the coulee bottom. This is a bad omen, he thinks.

The homestead crouches at the base of the coulee's north wall. From the ridge where he rides, it is nothing more than a warm shadow in the cool dark. The swollen river laps almost at the door. The man's descent is slow and guarded. He permits the horse a wide berth, and it picks its way reluctantly down. Gingerly like a new lover. The man dismounts before the gate, fashioned from timber and homespun twine. The knots are new. More clues. Signs he has collected like gifts. He ties the horse to a fence post, but his limbs are stiff from the riding and the cold and his fingers will not cooperate.

The yard leading to the sod hut is a swamp. He leans into each step, dragging the suck of his boots behind him. At the low door, he listens a moment and lifts the latch. A lone window allows the blue glow of moonlight into the kitchen. In one corner, a clay stove, a trunk, a dug-out tub, and a wooden bench. Across the room sit an anvil and a handmill, a rail table and chairs. Against one wall, there hang a flail, a scythe, and an axe. On the bench, carefully stored, smaller tools gather dust. A chisel, a plane drill, various hammers and files. On the table rest a lamp, a clay pot, and the remnants of a meal. Two place settings. This is all he needs.

The man draws his revolver. Holding it waist high and in front of him, he moves through the room. There is a drawn curtain at the far end. It is backlit from the only other window in the hut.

He stops long enough to pull back the hammer. It is the first sound he makes.

Seconds tick past. When he pushes through the cloth wall that hides the next room, everything is as he expects it. A bed against the wall. A body. He permits himself a smile for the first time in weeks. But something is missing. He should have noticed immediately, but the days of riding and rain have retarded his reflexes. The window is open. And next to it, partially obscured by the billowing cloth of the drapery, is the pale cream phosphorescent burn of a woman. She is naked. Her breasts are full and round. She is perfectly still. Her hair is the only thing that moves. And something else.

These are the misshappen pieces of a puzzle he has been assembling since Texas. He turns them over and over in his mind. And seconds tick past. But the pieces will not fit. He knows this before he begins the turning. He says something then, though he is not conscious of speaking. He has never moved so slowly.

The Wild Bunch

THE BOY ON THE RIDGE OF BLASTED ROCK CROUCHES STILL AS A gargoyle. The Great Northern Railway Train rushes toward him. In the last moments of repose before the locomotive barrels past, his body is in love with the earth. The stone cradles him like a lost bird. And then he is gone in a flutter of movement. A mass of coiled muscle released, Wyoming propels himself up and out into nothing. And in that brief instant, when he is suspended between earth and sky, there is real flight. A photograph then would reveal the span of his arms to be like wings. An x-ray would discover the delicate bones, the skeletal structure of trajectory. From the right distance, a man might say, "Look, there is a hawk." Or, "Do you see that sparrow?" Then the air gives way to the arc of his falling. His arms reach out, and he knows without searching where the guardrails will be. Gravity snatches at him like a hungry mouth. Pain rips through his limbs. The sinews of muscle tighten like rope. He bites down hard, but his hands hold. Adrenaline burns in his neck.

He looks backward then, over his shoulder in the whipping wind, to where Logan should be. The man's burly frame is twisting

11

oddly, awkwardly in a parody of flight. His arms stretch hopeful and desperate. But the angle is all wrong. Only a fault in the physics of collapse will save him. He crashes down on one side of the rail car and Wyoming feels the moment of impact rattle through his pelvis. The train holds the second man momentarily like an orbiting moon. And then he is mercury sliding backward into distance. It is the one arm flailing wildly that finds the guardrail in the end. But only by chance. His body has already disappeared over the edge. Wyoming recognizes from the irregular tilt of his weight that the arm has been ruined.

Sundance and Kilpatrick are like comets on horseback then, drawing alongside the train as it gathers steam. Logan launches his good arm onto the roof and heaves the bulk of his body to safety. Wyoming smiles, and throws the worried riders a wave as they pull away from the car. The relief is palpable. Logan bears down on the boy with hard grey eyes. But he is too late, and the look goes unnoticed. Wyoming is already moving forward, dancing over the back of the bullet beneath his feet.

When he reaches the coal tender, Wyoming should be able to see Butch and Deaf Charlie leaning on the horizon only a few hundred yards away. But his eyes are a terrible burden. At that distance the world is a small room in the bottom of a beer mug. Blurred and distorted. Behind him, Logan is struggling in the wind with one arm dangling useless at his side. Trees snap past like a nickelodeon possessed. Deftly Wyoming skips across the gap in the cars and clambers over the loose black rock. The train has crested the incline, and the riders fall back in the wake of its fresh speed. Without hesitation, Wyoming withdraws the long-barrelled Civil War pistol from its carriage beneath his arm. A handrail runs the length of the engineer's cabin, top to bottom. With the grace of a ballroom dancer, he holds the rail tightly in his hand and swings into the open door of the cabin. The driver retreats to the far side of the engine room. He opens his mouth, but no sound escapes.

"Sorry to intrude. But there'll be an unscheduled stop in today's run just a ways up the line. You see, this here's a holdup."

Ewen McGinnis is the one they call Wyoming. At twenty, he is by far the youngest of the Wild Bunch, and already he is famous among them. There is an energy and a restlessness about him that is contagious. He is so prolific and quick the ladies at Fanny Price's Sporting House offer him a discount. He is reckless and without fear. There seems no end to his good humour, and no limit to his ostentation. By eighteen, he is riding shotgun for Butch Cassidy and the most successful band of holdup men in the last half-century. He robs the bank at Winnemucca in his underwear.

The Wild Bunch give him the most dangerous work, not because he will do it, but because he will do it well. On the job, he drops out of the sky onto moving rail cars like cowboys drop into saddles. On the ground, he swaggers like a duck in boots too big for his feet, but on the top of a train he is fluid, liquid motion. A circus clown gone acrobat. He takes everything Logan teaches him and turns it into art. In another time, he might have been a celebrity. As it is, history will relegate him to the slush pile of unimportant things. There exist no photos of Wyoming. No home movies of his exploits on the railway. Nowhere does his name appear in print, but in the register of the Grand Hotel Vancouver, in British Columbia. In the narrative of outlaws, he will become redundant.

Wyoming was born on a dirt farm outside Omaha, Nebraska. His father was a veteran of the American Civil War who walked with a pronounced rolling gait. He had been wounded in the Wilderness fighting under Grant, and had received, upon discharge, a plot of land in the northern territory. He was a hardened man who was not afraid to live a hard life. But years of crop failure and harsh winters turned him onto drink. Twice he was incarcerated for discharging a weapon in a public place. Both times he had drunk himself close to blindness.

His young wife had several miscarriages before Wyoming. It was her death at the hands of pneumonia that caused him to give up drink and turn to God. Wyoming was not yet two years old. Despite the man's eventual reform, he was never able to lose the drunkard's reputation that hung about his neck like a noose until his own death fourteen years later. He would not remarry.

Wyoming was thrown out of the local school for persistent misbehaviour when he was only eight years old. He was taunted and teased. Students called him the stiller's son, and he learned to fight at an early age. Teachers just shook their heads and blamed it on the family.

"Shameful," they said. "A young boy running barefoot and wild with no mother to reign him in."

But the truth was that the boy could barely see what the teacher scratched into the board. Illiterate and poor, he roamed the county breaking windows, starting fights, and stealing chickens when he had the chance.

But in spite of his own reputation and the growing reputation of his son, each Sunday Wyoming's father dragged him to the little Catholic church—forlorn and peeling in the sun, or cold and moaning in the winter wind. Although he attended kicking and screaming, he was always, to a certain extent, in awe of the tiny services. The ostentatious cross above the altar. The rare occasion of incense in the air.

At fourteen, on a lark, Wyoming stole his first horse. His father was too poor to keep a proper mount, and yet riding came to the boy naturally. The boy's father, knowing the penalty for such an act, confessed to the crime himself. It was his last incarceration.

After his father's death Wyoming stole back the same horse and crossed the border into the state that would become his new home. On that lonesome journey, he took with him the only thing his father owned of any value. The forty-year-old .44 calibre Remington army revolver. Strapped to his chest by a length of binding twine.

The train comes to a stop above a small trestle where Butch has prepared the charge in anticipation. When the side wall of the Adams Express car tears off in the blast, the mess of tin and wooden planking flutters to the earth like a million butterflies. After the mistake in Wilcox on the Overland Flyer, Butch is careful with dynamite. Rattled by an obstinate rail guard, Butch had packed the charge with unnecessary zeal. When it blew, it tore the carriage in half. After that, the gang spent the better part of an hour gathering banknotes perched in trees. Logan thought to pistol-whip the guard, but Butch was pleased to see that the dynamite had not killed the blackened fellow, whose clothes were still smoking.

"Now, Harvey, a man with that kind of nerve deserves to be spared your pistol."

Butch steps through the matchsticks of the Great Northern Railway car to assess the safe, which is still intact.

"Pass me up that oil, will ya, Charlie."

Camillo Hanks pushes forward carrying a rubber canteen sack. The gang calls him Deaf Charlie on account of his one bad ear. He passes the sack, filled with nitroglycerin, to Butch. The week before, they teased Cassidy about the apron he wore while mixing the nitric acid with the sulphuric over a tub of crushed ice. Harvey told him that he would make someone a good wife some day, but that he was not much of a cook.

"And the soap, Charlie. If you please."

Butch sets to work on the safe. He plugs the cracks around the door with the softened washing soap, leaving a trough along the top. Into that, he pours the nitroglycerin mixture, which runs through the unseen channels. As a reflex, the other members move back into the brush. It is their first experience with the oil. Hanks sends a signal to Sundance and Kilpatrick, who are on the train, managing the passengers.

"Keep your head and hands inside the car," Sundance bellows up and down the line.

Just then a shot rings out from the area of the caboose. The outlaws drop in the undergrowth by the tracks. Sundance fires back, splintering the windowpane where the gunman's arm had been only a moment earlier. And as the gang eyes the caboose for any further action, a pistol is flicked through the same window. It rattles on the gravel like a toy.

Butch is moving backward through the rubble now, letting out fuse. He stops when he reaches the brush where Deaf Charlie and Harvey Logan stand with Wyoming. He searches the breast pocket of his horsehair vest for a match.

"Ladies and gentlemen. Behold the future of safe cracking."

Wyoming follows the consuming spark as it travels back through Butch's footsteps. A moment passes after it enters the safe. Chemicals break down, shift, and expand. The steam engine sighs, and then the pocket of silence that follows is blown open by the force of the explosion. The safe door, which had been quite immobile moments before, hurtles outward toward the men with astonishing velocity. And although it manages to miss each of the outlaws, it does pass dangerously close to Wyoming, severing a poplar directly behind. He is so slow to react, the tree reaches the earth before he does.

Butch is the first to speak.

"Somebody's like as not get themselves hurt if we keep that up."

Wyoming dusts himself off. Even Harvey Logan laughs.

From the beginning it was a race. The railway stitched its way onto the plains, infesting the western sprawl like metallic worms, resistant to the antibodies of the Jameses, the Youngers, and the last gasp of the Wild Bunch. The Union Pacific crawled in from the East and the Central Pacific slouched in from the Californian coast. Each of them just as hungry as the other for government money and land. A tidy sixty-four hundred hectares of federal land for every mile of track they put down. With the added bonus of sixteen thousand dollars per mile over flatlands, thirty-two thousand on the plateau, and forty-eight thousand once they hit the mountains. This more than doubles within the first year.

Every seventy miles gives birth to another boom town—Rawlins, Laramie, Cheyenne. And the white man pours in, displacing the Indian. Gobbles up more land. The buffalo, once thirty million strong, are hunted for fun and for trophy. The infamous hunter Frank Mayer called himself a harvester. He once bragged that the killing was so easy, he needed a canteen of water to cool down his barrel. And when he ran out of water, he resorted to piss. They use some of the meat to feed eleven thousand Chinese labourers, shipped in to help the Central Pacific break through the treacherous Sierra Nevada. The rest of the meat is left to rot in the grass. A similar fate befalls more than twelve hundred of the Oriental workers, buried under blasted rock or a sudden avalanche of snow.

The Cheyenne Indian. The Arapaho. The Lakota and the Sioux all do their best to turn back the clock. To stem the tides. But forts bloom out of the virgin soil to house troops. Resistance is an anachronism.

In 1893 at the Columbian exposition in Chicago, the frontier was declared officially closed. The winds of progress had triumphed. And in the pavilion that housed the state of Kansas, a herd of buffalo stood on display. Each one of them stuffed.

Wyoming met Sundance south of the Snake River at a ranch called the Crooked s. It was Sundance who showed him the world of the Outlaw Trail. Hole-in-the-Wall. Robber's Roost. Powder Springs. The Kid had been working the ranges of Baggs and Dixon since the spring of 1895. He was a legend *incognito*, and Wyoming knew him first as Harry Alonzo, common cowpoke. They worked together almost every day for a year. First, ear-marking calves, and alternately on roundup and drives. They spent money like time, and threw it away on the women and booze of Rock Springs or Thermopolis, and a series of railheads they happened across. The Kid was an uneasy surrogate father, but he enjoyed the wide-eyed adulation Wyoming offered him. The boy relished a good story, and once warmed to the idea, Sundance had a number to tell. He had not pulled a job in more than five years, but the itch was on him like a terrible bug. And the stories only made it worse.

Wyoming was there the night his cover was blown. The two men were in Tom Skinner's Saloon at Hog's Ranch. They had been drinking hard. Sundance was gambling and winning. One of the other players took exception. Words were exchanged. Accusations. The Kid was so fast off the draw, shooting was unnecessary. The gambler understood he was beaten before his hand hit the hilt of his gun. After that, there were no secrets between the Kid and Wyoming.

Sundance took the boy to the hideout in Hole-in-the-Wall after Wyoming was accused of stealing a horse. There he met George Curry and rode with the legend for a time during the Johnston County war. He would return later with the Wild Bunch. Using the secluded cabins as a base of operations.

Both Wyoming and Sundance were asked to stay on at the Crooked s for the winter of 1896. The work was slow and tedious. On the coldest days, Wyoming would take an axe out on the range to chop free the ice-covered watering holes. At other times, when the snow was too deep for grazing, he shovelled out hay to the herd. Once, he was badly frostbitten while rescuing stray yearlings caught along the fenceline during a storm. But for the most part, little happened in the way of excitement.

In April of the next year Curry came for the Kid. The long winter had worn Sundance down. He was ready for adventure. Told Wyoming about the bank in Belle Fourche, Dakota, before leaving. Without the older man's stories, Wyoming sought his own adventure, busting broncos for the range. It was a talent he was born to. After a year, his reputation was so widespread, Sundance had no problem locating him two years later when Butch Cassidy was working up a gang to tackle the Overland Flyer. Sundance gave him Wyoming. And the rest is history.

Harvey Logan is slowly getting drunk. Which is to say, he is getting mean. But Sundance is feeding him whiskey anyway. The outlaws concur that his shoulder is separated. The Kid intends to set it in place.

"Ready, Harve?"

"Ah, Jesus. Ain't there no other way?"

"Quit that awful bellyachin'. You're the biggest man in the room for crissakes, Harve."

"Gimme another slug of the whiskey."

"You've damn near drunk the bottle."

Harvey tips back the amber liquid with his one good arm. Wyoming is excited about the stacks of banknotes Hanks is counting on the table, but the spectacle of Logan's pain is too entertaining to extricate himself. He harbours a particular dislike for the man that goes back two years to Wilcox and the Overland Flyer—Wyoming's first run with the gang.

They are holed up in a cabin Kilpatrick scouted a week earlier. It is lost in the hills south of Malta, twenty miles from yesterday morning's holdup. It is a small farmhouse with a rotted-out pot-belly stove in one corner. The men can hear mice in the walls. Bird nests hang over their heads. The building is only one room, and but for two rickety chairs and a harvest table, no furniture is left behind. The front door is the only way in or out.

Butch paces the dirt floor. He sent Kilpatrick out for food and news more than an hour ago. Wyoming flips through a copy of *The Adventures of Billy the Kid*, staring at the pictures.

"Well, do you want the good news or the bad?"

Butch stops in the middle of the room and turns to Camillo Hanks, who has just spoken. Wyoming looks up from the magazine.

"The good," Butch decides.

"I count sixty-five thousand in banknotes."

The room is quiet. Hanks has a particular light in his eye. Wyoming looks to Butch for a reaction. The man's suspenders are down around his knees. His chest is bare.

"Well, I'll be jiggered. We've yet to match that. Whatta ya say, Kid?"

"That's the biggest take. Easy."

"Jesus, Wyoming. You can afford to get yerself a decent pair of boots," spits Logan.

"What's wrong with my boots?"

"Nothin'. If yer expectin' to grow into 'em."

Wyoming stands before Logan with his legs spread wide.

"Now, Ewen, just sit down."

"But Butch, he's pokin' fun at my feet."

"Well, son. They are a little small."

"And you know what they say about the size of a man's feet."

While Harvey is still laughing, Sundance picks up the man's damaged arm and pulls it into place in one fluid motion. The grinding cartilage sounds like a Venetian card shuffle.

"Good fuckin' Christ."

Wyoming looks down with a smile at the man writhing on the floor.

"You okay, Harve?"

"Shut up, you little Irish dwarf. I swear to God I'm gonna shoot you."

"Leprechaun, Harve. Leprechaun." Sundance tips the last slug of whiskey into his mouth.

"What the hell d'you do that fer, Kid?"

"Fuck, Harve," Sundance responds, wiping the back of his sleeve over his lips. "The thing was useless to you that way. It needed to be set right."

"How d'you know what's got to be done? You ain't no doctor."

"No. But I shot one once. And that makes me more qualified than anyone else in the room."

"Christ. You're as thick as Wyoming."

"Careful, Harve. I ain't got no druthers 'bout shootin' patients, neither."

Butch steps between the quarrelling men.

"Awright, the both of you shut up. Charlie, what's the bad news?"

"The notes. They ain't signed, Butch."

"That ain't bad news. When we get them back to Powder Springs, we'll have Bill Carver do 'em up. He's got a good hand."

The room goes quiet in the wake of Butch's declaration.

"But, Butch. Quickdraw was shot down in Sonora a few months back."

"Oh. Well, we'll get Elzy Lay then."

"He's got life in New Mexico for shootin' Sheriff Eddy Farr."

"Ketchum?"

"Dead."

"Jesus. Then we'll get Etta to sign them. She's still alive, ain't she, Kid?"

"Why don't we give Wyoming a turn?" Logan interjects.

The boy's face flushes red. It's all he can do not to kick Logan where he lies. But Kilpatrick throws open the door then. His eyes go straight to Butch.

"What is it?"

"Read for yerself."

He tosses a copy of the *Grand Falls Tribune* among the stacks of neatly piled banknotes. Hanks gathers it up.

Great Northern Hit By Wild Bunch

JULY 3, 1901, WAGNER—The infamous Wild Bunch have done it again. Yesterday afternoon at approximately 2:00 pm, the Great Northern Railway Train was stopped outside Wagner, Montana, by a band of gunmen believed to include Butch Cassidy, Kid Curry, The Tall Texan, Deaf Charlie and The Sundance Kid. A sixth outlaw was identified by different sources as Walt Putney or Matt Warner.

"That's you, Wyoming. Golly you're famous."

"Harvey, if you don't shut up, I'll shoot you myself," Butch interjects. "Go on, Charlie."

Daredevil Butch Cassidy leapt from a rock ledge onto the roof of the dining car as the train gathered steam. "He dropped into the cabin cool as a cucumber. He had a gun on me, but the man was polite," said the train's engineer, William Durban.

The room is a tunnel of laughter. Butch looks to Wyoming with a crooked smile.

Dynamite was used to access the Express car, but the criminals employed nitroglycerin when opening the safe. The take is estimated at more than $40,000.

"These outlaws won't get far," said an official from the North Pacific Railway. "We've hired 100 independent law officers to track them down." According to the railroad, Charles Sirango of the Pinkerton Detective

Agency has been employed to oversee the capture of the holdup men. The first posse left the county seat at Glasgow only hours after the holdup. In addition, Wyoming lawman, Joe Lefors, says that he will be waiting at the border, and that no member of the Wild Bunch will find refuge in that state.

This is the second time that the Wild Bunch has chosen the Great Northern line. Residents will remember the holdup east of Malta nine years ago now.

"Did he say one hundred officers?"

"I think they're from Pinkerton's, Butch."

"And Sirango too?"

"So it says."

"How the hell did the news get out so fast?" Wyoming blurts.

"It's that damn telegraph." Butch looks to Hanks, who still holds the paper. "What's this world coming to? How's a man supposed to make a living?"

Butch sits down at the table across from Hanks. His head is heavy with thought. He uses his hands to support it. The whole room, including Wyoming, tries not to stare at him. It is always like this. Each of them has an idea. Maybe the same one. But no one acts before Butch. It is not fear, but a matter of respect. Wyoming leans against the door frame.

Butch speaks, "Ben, you get enough food for the trail?"

The Tall Texan nods in response.

"We leave now. If Sirango is in charge, they'll already be riding. We'll have to make the Black Hills before dark."

He looks to Wyoming and offers him a wink. The boy sees right through it.

Wyoming cannot blame Butch for the article. That's the way the newsmen wanted him. Larger than life. An American Robin Hood standing in the way of the railway machine. The eastern cattle companies that were closing down the West and squeezing out the dirt farmers of Nebraska and the ranchers of Brown's Park, Utah. Johnston County, Wyoming.

Two years ago, Wyoming actually believed Butch was larger than life. When he got off his horse to shake the boy's hand, he had a grin wider than the Mississippi River Delta. Wyoming was convinced that he could talk a nun out of her habit. He was not much taller than Sundance. They even looked alike. But where the Kid was dark and moody, Butch was bright and energetic. Electricity burned in the grip of his fist. To Wyoming, the man was a giant.

Butch needed a sixth man for the Wilcox heist he had been planning. He ran the most successful holdup gang in the history of the United States, so of course the boy was flattered to have been considered. Enamoured even. The three of them rode into Powder Springs for a drink and stayed three days. Butch drank so much his mind was erased. He forgot the boy's name on the evening of the second day and called him Wyoming for the duration of their stay. The name followed him thereafter. Wyoming did not have the courage to tell Butch that he was actually from outside Omaha. But in the end, Wyoming rang sweeter than Nebraska.

Butch never officially asked him to join the Bunch. He did not consider the gang as "his." It was an amorphous body of criminals and cowboys that gravitated to the man's charm. They liked the way he spoke. They respected the way he thought. But most of all they liked him because he was a man of perpetual motion. The action was never far off when Butch was around. So it did not seem odd or out of place to anyone concerned when Wyoming followed the outlaws to Wilcox to rob the Overland Flyer.

The outlaws move through the landscape at a quick trot, riding single file to disguise their numbers and to blaze only a weak trail. The horses are fresh and of superior quality. If the posse comes across the cabin where they spent the night, it will find only the plugs used during the holdup grazing in the fields. Wyoming is atop a blue roan now. A mustang with strong sloping shoulders and sure feet. The gang tack southwest around Fort Peck Lake in the direction of Great Falls. It is a necessary evil. No one has discussed the path they will ride once they have crested the western line of the lake, but the unspoken fear among them is a second posse, trekked out to Billings by rail. Once over the Marias, Hole-in-the-Wall is three days' hard ride to the southeast over bitter plateaux.

Butch and Sundance trot ahead of the band, locked in serious debate. Wyoming is bunched together with Logan and Hanks. Kilpatrick brings up the rear, scanning the scorched earth for signs of pursuit.

The Bunch wends a circuitous trail over injured country ruined by sun. The beargrass rattles, nothing but dry husks in the breeze. Although now and again, they pass resilient patches of purple larkspur and the orange heat of Indian paintbrush among tracts of uninterrupted sagebrush. They take great pains to disperse their scent in the many creeks and coulees along their tempered descent toward the river valley they must ford. After Wilcox, they were set upon by dogs shipped in from Omaha, and the memory is still fresh with Wyoming.

Like this, they ride into the slow clock of afternoon heat, every now and again sending a rider on a false loop to the east or to the west in an effort to slow down and divide the strength of the Pinkerton posse, which floats unseen like heat waves on the plain behind them.

It is Kilpatrick who sounds the alarm just after the Marias appears like a dumb snake below them. Although Wyoming can see nothing, Hanks pulls up short and confirms that there is a dust cloud kicking in the north. It is still several miles behind, but closing fast. The Bunch slows up at the banks of the river. There is no way to know if they too have been seen.

Wyoming and the others forded here on their hike into Wagner a week earlier, and before long they pick their way quickly across. The water's cool chant is refreshing. Wyoming's forearms are covered in scrapes and needles from the cloying sagebrush and thickets. An upturned wagon lies silting off the opposite shore.

They rally their horses on the far bank.

"If we head for Hole-in-the-Wall now, we might as well turn ourselves in," Butch spits. "They're like as not to have a regulation chuck riding along with 'em. Which means enough food and water for the whole posse and their horses to boot. But it'll slow 'em down."

The great bay Butch is riding can sense the man's mood swing and refuses to sit still, kicking and spinning in the dust. Wyoming is never much worried about anything, but the look in Butch's eyes as his horse dances in the dirt reminds him of their predicament in Wilcox.

"We can't be sure what's waitin' for us on the trail south, but if I know Sirango, he'll of had a posse leave Billings not long after this Glasgow pack. Our best shot is to lose these bulls in the foothills of the Bearpaws." Butch looks to the men for their opinions as though he is unsure himself.

"Wherever we go, it'll be a hard ride and we'll need new horses before we hit the mountains," adds Sundance.

"We'll pick some up around Lewistown," Logan offers. "I know some people."

The agreement is wordless. Wyoming kicks his horse in the direction of the sinking sun, and the Bunch is off at a terrible speed, scrabbling up the riverbank and over the high plain with the Pinkerton posse homing in from the north.

Allen Pinkerton came to America with a warrant over his head and eventually founded the largest detective agency in the United States. History is not without its sense of irony. The Scottish barrel maker settled in the small town of Dundee, Illinois, in 1843 and literally stumbled over his first criminal conspiracy—the smoking remains of a bonfire on a nearby island. Exercising his soon-to-be-famous sense of intuition, the man staked out the empty encampment in his spare time. Like a divining rod for criminal activity, Pinkerton's nose managed to sniff out a band of counterfeiters minting phony coins.

After several other unlikely incidents, word spread like fire through sagebrush, and soon Pinkerton had established a reputation for himself. Within a year, Chicago called and he became the city's first full-time detective. But as a man trained to stop bungholes, he began to notice the gaping cracks in the country's law enforcement system. And in 1850, he set out to fill them by way of the Pinkerton National Detective Agency.

Police forces on the American frontier were particularly disorganized, notoriously understaffed, and gloriously underpaid. The climate was ripe for corruption. And in towns like Deadwood, Dodge, and Tombstone, lawlessness prevailed.

More often than not, the line between outlaw and lawman was no thicker than the width of a tin star. Every county had an elected sheriff, who might or might not have an undersheriff at his disposal, and every town had a marshal with a small police force in relation to its size. But both the sheriff and the marshal reserved the right to deputize just about any yahoo off the range who owned a gun and was able to handle a horse. A man who was deputy one day, might have been the man hunted the next.

More importantly, the sheriffs and the marshals responsible for upholding laws in the West often had unique views on the way these laws were interpreted and enforced. In fact, many a marshal, and more than a few sheriffs, came from retired or reformed criminal stock. Those being the men the populations trusted to best handle their former compatriots. Wyatt Earp is a shining example of a one-time horse thief gone straight—or at least not entirely crooked.

The fact of the matter is, sheriffs and marshals made steady, but often small, salaries. Yet through their collection of taxes and handling of county contracts, including road building, they were often able to retire wealthy. Earp, for instance, lived comfortably to 1929 off mining investments purchased with the money he skimmed as an officer of the peace.

But no other marshal tread so easily back and forth over that imaginary line as one Wild Bill Hickok. A man who spent more time in liquor halls and gambling establishments than he did patrolling the streets. And no matter what fabrications—introduced by the press or by himself—were added to his reputation as a gunslinger, it cannot be argued that more than one man was cut down by his twin set of six-guns. Many of those while he sported a star.

But it is also true that in a world where lawlessness prevailed for at least one generation, the actions and ideals of a man standing alone against the rising tide cannot be expected to hold up under close scrutiny.

However, in spite of this corruption it was the railroads that stood first in line for the Pinkerton services, and not the municipalities. The "Pinks," as they became known, would pursue a man from one end of the country to another. Just the sort of agents needed to protect the railroads' interests, which stretched across the continent like brittle limbs.

But more important than the flexibility of its operatives was the agency's Scottish penchant for immaculate records. Pinkerton invented the mug shot and soon amassed the world's largest collection of criminal portraiture. A compilation of artwork to rival the Louvre. They diligently scanned the newspapers of every hick and boom town from New York to Los Angeles, clipping stories and scrawling notations in the margins. They had enough paperwork to write the life stories of every two-bit thief and amateur forger in the country. This way investigative innovation unfurled itself into the frontier like flypaper.

The Pinkertons eventually became as famous as the criminals they pursued—the James Boys, the Youngers, the Renos, and the Farringtons. And, it should be noted, despite the magnesial flashes of such characters in the history of America, it was the dogged and relentless pursuit of the Pinkertons that won out in the end.

Robert Pinkerton—Allen's youngest son—made his career off the backs of the James and Younger gangs. He and his men tore up the states of Missouri, Kentucky, Kansas, and Minnesota while running down the bandits. Never offering a moment's reprieve.

Their constant clashing ballooned into a war all its own. Each of them trying to outdo the other in the papers. Playing up to the public thirst for action and adventure. The copy practically wrote itself.

In 1874 Jesse James and Clell Miller kidnapped the Pinkerton agent Joseph W. Pilcher and turned him into a martyr for the company. At a crossroads in Independence, Missouri, they shot him dead and threw his body down like a line in the sand, at the same location of an earlier shootout with the agency. In retaliation, the Pinks tracked down John Younger and killed him in return.

The Pinkerton information machine was so dependable and quick in its dissemination of warnings and tip-offs that eventually it seemed they knew where the James and Younger gangs meant to strike next, before Jesse or Frank had decided. It was Pinkerton information that allowed the townspeople of Northfield, Minnesota, to ambush the gang in a botched robbery attempt. Many of the bandits were captured or killed, and it was only dumb luck that allowed Frank to drag the wounded body of Jesse down to the healing waters of the Missouri River, where they stole a skiff and escaped.

The disappearance of the Jameses and Youngers was but a foreshadowing of the agency's next love affair with the Wild Bunch, as the operatives stretched their influence westward. Ever westward.

The Rocky Mountains prop up the western rim of Montana like a lean-to shed, and the rest of the state slopes away east into the Missouri River Basin. Wyoming does not know the badlands of Montana like he knows the country of the Big Horn Mountains, but he does know that every mile of caked earth they spit back into dust on their way to the Bearpaws is another mile away from the safe haven of Hole-in-the-Wall and their eventual return to Brown's Hole or Powder Springs.

The outlaws arrive at a ranch outside Lewistown in a racket of hoof beats, snorting, and exploding earth. The horses are foaming and bloody from spurs. Logan and Butch speak with the owner, who eyes the gang closely, but eventually strikes a deal. They act quickly and efficiently but, doubtless, they lose much of the distance gained in their manic afternoon ride as they saddle the new mounts and redistribute the gear.

Wyoming urges his fresh buckskin mare mercilessly into the twilight. They reach the foothills of the Bearpaw range as the sun is setting, but aside from the scattered stands of lodgepole pine, the hills offer little shelter. They climb at a good pace until dark. It is not until sparks fly from the horseshoes that the outlaws come spontaneously to a rest. The hoof beats on loose shale and scree are as good as a signpost, ringing out their arrival in the mountains. Thick glades of shaggy trees now populate the hillside. The wake of their run is swallowed by night.

The six men lean forward in their saddles. Wyoming pants in time with the animal beneath him. Sundance is the first to speak.

"They can't follow us through the night, Butch. We ain't eat since dawn, and this climbing has worked an evil on the horses."

"I think mine throwed a shoe just now, when we hit the rock," says Hanks.

"How's the shoulder, Harve?"

"Fine, Butch. But I'm with the Kid. We oughta make camp."

"Okay. We'll bed down here, just beyond those trees. Charlie, you hobble the horses and make sure that they get some water."

Wyoming pats the beast beneath his saddle.

"See if you can't fill the canteens too. Lord knows we'll need it for tomorrow."

The men crouch on their haunches or lounge against the rugged pine. No one speaks for a long time. After a while, Butch sends Wyoming to look for the posse. The boy picks his way down over the loose shale and through the thick batches of bracken littering the hillside. Over the first rise, even his eyes cannot mistake the hot tongues of the Pinkerton fires in the lower part of the range. He scampers back up the hill to Butch.

"They're holed up in a gully. They've set fires. We're safe for tonight."

"We'll have to post a watch. We can't let them get the jump."

The men sit down to dried meat and bread for supper. Butch doesn't allow for a fire. When Charlie returns with the water, Logan is sent off for the first watch.

Hanks asks, "What do we do now, Butch?"

"The way I see it, we got two options. Just over these hills, there's a mountain trail that goes through Two Bridges and Dillon. Me and the Kid used it once coming north outa Idaho. It'll take us clear into Utah and we can make for The Roost or stop at some place a little less obvious."

"What's the other option?" says Kilpatrick in his slow Texas drawl.

"We can turn east and make a run for it over the plains north of Billings and take our chances in the Bighorn Basin. We got friends at Hog's Ranch what could give us fresh horses and a spot to lie low. No matter what, we can't hide out in these mountains. There ain't enough food and water."

"What if we split up?"

A pause enters the conversation like a door jamb after Sundance speaks. Wyoming has been dreading the suggestion since morning. Still its arrival turns his blood cold.

"Yeah. I was thinking that," says Butch.

Wyoming draws a line in the earth. Without the help of the moon, Butch cannot see the look on his face. But the boy knows that he will be staring.

Wyoming considers the outlaw life to be one of extremes, much like the landscape he inhabits. In the same way a blasted plateau can suddenly rocket upward into the crooked finger of Devil's Tower, a life of leisurely decadence can explode in an unexpected adrenaline rush of cat and mouse. He never has been one for the decadence, always craving the next run. The heist. Quietude unsettles him.

It is for this reason that he looks fondly upon his memories of the cowboy life. The life he spent with Sundance and others. The life he had before this one. Were it not for the monotony of winters, he might never have left it. It was a hard life, but one of constant activity, and danger, if in smaller measure than his new profession. The current enticement of that life being a distinct lack of Harvey Logans. Men who confuse courage for the readiness to kill.

Life on the drive is characterized by grumbling and cursing, but underwritten with stoic toughness. Wyoming has passed many a night into dawn on the back of a horse, and then ridden another twelve-hour day. He has slogged three days without much more than stale bread and coffee, and still pulled cattle from sinkholes of mud. Fended off prairie wolves with a six-gun. At times the blackflies were so bad, he couldn't see the ass of the steer in front of him.

Once the herd he was driving out of Gillette ate up a field of locoweed. The cattle threw hallucinogenic fits and foamed at the mouth. Several groaned through the night and died in the morning. Others had to be shot or tracked down and dragged in unconscious.

And always the silent threat of Indian raiding parties clouded the horizon as the drive skirted tribal lands.

Sometimes Wyoming could hardly think, he was so bonded to the moment with labour and diligence. But he knows now, as he reflects on those hard days in batwing chaps or woollies, that he was living. Really living. At every turn. Now he runs in jerks and fits and starts, and wonders if that is enough. If it's right.

The Pinkerton Detective Agency carved up the bandits of the West and stuck them into boxes. Naming the enemy was an early priority. It removed him from the realm of the unknown— painted a face on the bogeyman. To begin, there were thieves, and there were killers. The latter was a smaller group, if a more dangerous one. The Pinks offered these men little respect. Hunted them down like rabid animals. Just as happy to see them dead as behind bars. Men who were damned anyway. Men like Billy the Kid and John Wesley Hardin. The agency was supported by the American public in its campaign. Neither having any other cure for a scourge of their kind but to rub them out entirely like scratch off a slate.

The thieves were further subdivided into rustlers and robbers. The former being as near to untouchable as possible. The tracks of unmarked pasture were too vast, and the practice of the open range made it almost impossible to protect unbranded mavericks. All a rustler had to do was separate enough heads and make for the lawless folds of Starr Valley, Powder Springs, or any other isolated hideout with access to water and food for the herd. Lawmen had learned not to enter these havens after brushes in Hole-in-the-Wall and other bandit hideouts. A winter in one of these prosperous valleys would fatten the herd, and in the spring, a brand of the rustlers' choosing would be applied to the steers. Rustling was as respectable as any other profession in the West.

And so it was to the robbers that the Pinks looked to make
their reputation. Greater in number and as prolific as rabbits.
Springing up in every cow and rail town east of the Mississippi.
For them, the agency created a hierarchy of criminal nomencla-
ture. Yeggmen. Sneak thieves. Forgers. And at the top of this
dubious folio—the holdup man.

Yeggmen were fleas in the Pinkerton pelt. Men who posed like
beggars and drifters, and were little more than that anyway.
Wafting into boom towns, checking things out, and making men-
tal notes about everything from street lighting to escape routes.
These men scratched out an existence on the bravura of others.
Coughing up their information for pennies from any eventual
take. Sneak thieves, on the other hand, tended to be con men.
Unlucky card sharps with a talent for talking. These men often
worked in teams, robbing bank safes and retail chips, while one of
their sorry band drew attention to himself and away from his dex-
trous compatriots. Forgers, however, were men of intelligence,
money, and a certain degree of talent. At least the scratcher anyway. The one who made the necessary plates. The one who performed the art. Again, these men worked in teams with a financial
backer, middlemen, and presenters.

However, no outlaws received more attention than the bright
stars of the holdup men. Men like Butch and Sundance, and even
Wyoming. Their antics mirrored the pioneering spirit of the
West. Men who stood up to banks from the East and railroad
land barons intent on the best parcels of arable property. Their
success depended on a modicum of talent, but drew much more
heavily on a windfall of balls. The pressmen made love to their
exploits—rightly or wrongly—and somewhere deep inside, the
attraction was mutual. Moth and flame in symbiotic expression.
For many of these men were the former adrenaline junkies of the
Confederate Army. And later they were the sons of dirt farmers
itchy with the stasis of life on the plains, or labourers tired of the
dust and terror of life in the mines.

These men lived out the vicarious wishes of a frontier nation running quickly out of room.

Butch got his start the same way Wyoming got his. Through theft. Only Robert Leroy Parker—Butch's real name—stole a saddle and left the horse to its own devices. And unlike Wyoming's, Parker's father was not about to confess to the crime. The brief stint he would spend in the county jail would be Parker's only time spent behind bars in a life that exemplified the outlaw way.

After his release, he followed rustler Mike Cassidy, a former employee on his father's ranch, into the Henry Mountains not far from the Colorado River. The two men worked up their own herd of cattle by scouring the mountains for unmarked mavericks, and then branding them illegally. Parker was so fond of his mentor and this new way of life that he kept the older man's name when he struck out on his own.

Like many other Utah youths, he initially tried to make his fortune in the mines opened around Telluride. But there he met Matt Warner, another outlaw, who eventually dubbed the boy Butch, after he tricked him into firing a needle gun of the same nickname. The recoil of the gun sent Cassidy flying several yards backward into a water hole for cattle. Thus, when he finally hit the Outlaw Trail in earnest, Robert Leroy Parker was already commonly known as Butch Cassidy.

Butch came from strong stock. In fact his whole family passed through the same forbidding mountain ranges that he would later return to and make his home. Only they passed through them in search of Zion, not loose mavericks and payroll shipments. His people were Mormons too poor to purchase oxen and horses. But that did not stop them from clambering after their decided prophet,

Brigham Young. Instead, they walked the distance from the banks of the Missouri River, through the high mountain country of South Pass, Wyoming, and down again into the deserts of Utah. Earning themselves the title of the Handcart Pioneers of 1856.

The majority of them left late in the year, placing their trust in God. However, He rewarded their trust in October with snow squalls and high winds. Many died on the trail through South Pass, and many more in Martin's Hollow. One of the troop's stalwart leaders was the formidable Robert Parker. A man who refused to let snowdrifts past his head slow the procession until spring. He blazed a trail through the mountains and pulled all his family's worldly possessions behind him like a beast of burden. With the worst behind him, Robert Parker took it upon himself to die quietly in his sleep, a few miles from the promised land.

The widow Parker and her son, Maximilian, did eventually make it to Salt Lake City. But Maxie would eventually turn around and repeat the journey several times over, guiding emigrant trains on behest of the church. He would also fight in the Blackhawk War and help raise the fort at Panguitch. But, arguably, his most famous accomplishment would be the conception of a son. One Robert Leroy Parker. A different sort of prophet.

It is Sundance who stirs before dawn. Light has not entered the world.

"They're on the move. Fire's out."

The members of the Wild Bunch climb under cover of trees for the first part of the morning, taking refuge in the sheltered hollows of the Bearpaw Mountain Range. But eventually they are forced onto an exposed cliff face high above the valley floor. The men from Pinkerton's are crawling after their trail through the bush like fleas in a dog's coat.

"Jesus. There must be more than twenty of them down there."

"Guess we ain't lost them neither. They're moving right along the path we come up."

"Yeah. But they ain't got no more chuck. We're on even ground now."

An eagle wings past during their ascent, and at one point Wyoming spots a wolf flash in the trees. The ground beneath his feet is old. Granite outcrops rubbed clean of soil and moss. Tree roots clinging precariously to life.

The outlaws camp again that evening, but this time Sundance sounds the alarm in the middle of the night. The fires are out. The posse stirs. Determined to wear down the outlaws, it seems.

It is another day of hard climbing before they crest the hills and begin their descent toward the Musselshell River. They have done the better part of the climb on foot, but can now use the horses again. A narrow valley spreads beneath them, running east and west.

"They ain't give up yet, Butch. Any normal posse'd of give by now," says Wyoming. The men from Pinkerton's are professionals. He knows their reputations well. What they did to the James Gang. The Youngers. What they have begun to do in the West.

"These is paid hunters," replies Harvey.

"Listen," interjects Butch. "We ain't got much of a choice, now. Once we hit that valley floor, we're gonna have to split up. Me and the Kid and Deaf Charlie will head southwest into Idaho like I said. We done it before. Only in reverse. Logan, you take Ben and Wyoming—"

"Oh, Christ."

"Now listen, Harve. He knows the Bighorn country better than you do. And if there's a posse waitin' you'll need his gun."

"I ain't ridin' with him, Butch."

The others stare at Wyoming. There is a history between the two men. This much they know.

"I ain't," the boy repeats.

"Now listen, Ewen. I'm the leader of this here parade. We

ain't gonna stop at all tonight. When we hit that valley floor, we'll split the cash and ride through till dawn. I ain't takin' any chances. We'll meet up in Fort Worth and get these notes properly doctored. Then me and the Kid are through, and you guys can fight it out amongst yerselves."

It is not the first time Wyoming has heard Butch use that phrase. He and Sundance have been planning their escape for more than a year. He has heard talk of Australia. South America. Even Canada.

Soon there will be nothing left of the frontier. No place left to hide. There is no room for men like Butch and Sundance in the new vision of America.

It is a long slow ride down with only a new moon to guide them.

The Outlaw Trail stretched four thousand miles over the most desperate landscape between Canada and Mexico. It went its way through the plateaux of Montana, into the mountains of Idaho, Wyoming, and Colorado, and through the deserts of Utah, Nevada, Arizona, and New Mexico. The topography of that area was ideal for thieves, robbers, holdup men, and murderers. Before the 1860s, it was still virgin territory, visited only by fur trappers and adventurers. And even after the railway penetrated its shell, the harsh climate, run through with deserts, mountains, and unfathomable canyons, turned back the majority of sodbusters, or sent them over the hills to the coast.

A seasoned outlaw with a keen knowledge of the dim trails and hidden water holes could disappear from the law and subsist for weeks and even months in the tangle of wilderness. The Trail was a legend in its own time. A magnet for the worst element of society. There were so many bandits on the Trail during this period that their crimes reached new heights of daring and spectacle.

Headquarters sprung up in Brown's Hole, Robber's Roost, and Hole-in-the-Wall, along with scores of other less important hideouts. Their locations, although famous, were almost inaccessible. Brown's Hole straddled the borders of Utah, Colorado, and Wyoming, which confused the jurisdictions of all three law enforcement agencies. It was practically impregnable at the bottom of a walled canyon in the Uintah Mountains. And yet the valley floor was rich and fertile, running thirty miles along the muddy waters of the Green River. It was perfect for rustlers who knew the area and could sneak in a herd of unmarked mavericks. They might actually winter there protected from the harsh winds, fattening their newfound herds, and then run them north to a railhead. With South Pass and Atlantic City booming as gold towns, all kinds of gamblers and thieves were already in the area. Eventually it became the cattle-rustling capital of Wyoming. Outlaws like Valentine Hoy, Buckskin Ed, and the Speckled Nigger made their reputations there.

And naturally, with a reputation like that, it was the first place Butch Cassidy went following his release from the Wyoming pen. He even built his own hideout on a sandstone outcropping and invited the likes of Elzy Lay, Matt Warner, and Bob Meeks to ride into history with him. Their antics and adventures at Brown's Hole were what earned the gang its eventual moniker.

Robber's Roost, unlike Brown's Hole, was neither walled nor in the mountains. Instead, it sat openly on the elevated plains of southern Utah. But it was a forbidding, isolated place of sparse vegetation and ruined earth. Travellers and lawmen could be seen from miles away. It was first used as a hideout in 1883 by rough men like George Curry and the deadly McCarty Brothers. But when Cassidy and the Wild Bunch blew in after the Castle Gate payroll job, the whole area took on an aristocratic air. The men had money and weren't afraid to throw it around. They even built a second hideout in the shadow of the Orange Cliffs and lived like kings until the money went dry.

Hole-in-the-Wall, on the other hand—the most northern

headquarters, in Johnston County, Wyoming—was a place of absolute myth. Accessible only by a cart-sized break in the brilliant red sandstone cliffs near the K-C Ranch. A handful of well-armed bandits could hold off an army from this position. The James Brothers and Big Nose George are only a sampling of the bandits who held out in Hole-in-the-Wall—also known simply as Outlaw Ranch. During the Johnston County War, a small number of cattle rustlers turned back an invasion of lawmen. An event in Wyoming's history second only to Custer's Last Stand.

Like Brown's Hole, behind the red sandstone cliffs lay miles and miles of rolling pasture land. And with Deadwood, South Dakota, just a stone's throw away, the combination of bad characters and opportunity was positively electric. But it wasn't until a natural disaster—namely an abnormally cold winter in 1887—wiped out ninety percent of the steer herds in Johnston County that the true outlaw age came to Hole-in-the-Wall. Hundreds of unemployed cowboys were set free on the range as a result, and more than a few of them were ready to double as rustlers and thieves to make up for lost wages.

It was around this time that the Logan Brothers rode into town and hooked up with the already infamous George Curry. In late 1887 Curry and the Logans led a band of almost seventy outlaws from Hole-in-the-Wall down to another hideout in Powder Springs, where the Wild Bunch happened to be staying. A fellow by the name of Harry Longabaugh was among them. A relatively unknown thief from Sundance, Wyoming. Thus the Train Robbers' Syndicate came into being.

And it was into this world of action and adventure that one eighteen-year-old Ewen McGinnis found himself pulled like a magnet. He would soon discover that while heroism and bravery did exist on the Outlaw Trail—chivalry and bravado—a deep running undercurrent of desperation and depravity existed in disproportionate measure. And only in this world could the Butch Cassidys and the Harvey Logans meet and call themselves friends.

Butch is a wrinkle fending off time. He is not the man Wyoming
met two years ago. Rumours twist like snakes among the rough
men. It has been said that he contacted Judge Powers. That a deal
was struck with the railroad. Some say it was a hoax. Others say
the deal fell through. That they left him like a sitting duck, holed
up in Utah.

Wyoming half believes the stories. But they do not lower his
estimation of the man. Butch always has one ear to the ground.
He knows that the railroad is closing fast. Rumbling in the distance. When it comes to the railway, Butch sides with the Indian.
It has closed up the last vestiges of wilderness like a series of zip-
pers, stitching the country together. Shrinking the West.

But unlike the other bandits who have fallen victim to time,
Butch is a strain adapting to drugs. After a bank robbery in Montpellier, he rides a train clear into Iowa and then north to Chicago,
as an honest-to-goodness paying customer. Posses are tearing up
the trails in his absence—hunting for ghosts—while Butch
attends a performance of *The Importance of Being Earnest* at the
Ontario Theatre. He wears new clothes and a fresh derby hat
purchased at Roebucks. The next day he reboards the train for
Bay City, Michigan, and finds work as a deckhand on the
schooner *The Eagle*. When he leaves the riverboat at Sandusky, he
is picked up by a travelling circus. By the time he returns to
Wyoming, his death has been mistakenly reported in the papers.
But how long can a man run?

Butch is not stupid. He knows when the game is up. He is
making alternative plans. Setting aside cash. On the night before
Wagner, he takes the boy aside.

"You ought to think about Canada, kid. The West is a vise, and
somebody's turning the screw."

Wyoming does not have the opportunity to say goodbye to Butch before they are riding again. A glance is all he exchanges with the man. All the memory he takes with him. The square jaw set in stone. The happy eyes under bleached brows and lashes. And the derby hat. Slightly aslant like a final salute. And he knows the world is changing. Stretching out in unknown directions.

When the sun comes up, there is no sign of the posse. He is thankful for this, until he digests the position of the dawn. They are moving northeast, and not south.

"Harve, you got us all turned around," he says.

The big man pulls up short. Kilpatrick is silent, looking away.

"I ain't fool enough to pass that close to Billings," Harvey snaps.

"But Butch said to—"

"I don't answer to Butch no more, kid. We've got our share of the loot. What we do now is our business."

Wyoming looks to Kilpatrick. His tall lanky body is uneasy in the saddle.

"Are you in this with him, Ben? He's takin' us back north for crissakes."

"I reckon he'll be in Argentina before we ever get to Fort Worth," the tall man drawls, referring to Butch.

Wyoming looks to Logan and back to Kilpatrick again.

"Well then, give me my share. I ain't afraid of no posses outa Billings."

"It don't work that way, kid," Logan laughs. "I can't afford to have you rat me out to the authorities when yer caught. If you want yer money, you'll have to follow me."

"You're takin' us right back to where we started!"

"That's right. No posse'd ever figure on that one. Once we're clear of Billings, we'll light out back down south, straight for Hole-in-the-Wall. We'll avoid the Bighorn Gulch altogether. And besides, I have a little business that needs attending back this way." Harvey ends the discussion by urging his sorrel plug around with his thighs.

"What does he mean by 'unfinished business'?"

"I couldn't tell ya, kid," Ben answers. "He had a girl up this way. But that was a long time ago."

"Are you ladies comin' or not?" shouts Logan over his shoulder.

"Ain't you the least bit concerned?"

"I'm more concerned about bein' shot by Kid Curry," Kilpatrick says as he nudges his horse into line with Logan's.

The first time Wyoming saw a man killed, it was at the hands of Harvey Logan. The Wilcox getaway had been a fiasco. Two separate posses rode out of Medicine Bow and Dana, tipped off by the telegraph. They were joined by a special rail car of marshals and bloodhounds the next day. It was raining hard and the North Platte River was in flood. Butch had the Bunch scatter and Wyoming ended up in a cabin in Casper Creek with Logan and Flat-Nosed Curry. Word came that Sheriff Joe Hazen was on to them, and the three were forced into a flat open ride on the Salt Creek Road. The posse was so close, Wyoming could hear the snorting of their horses. The outlaws were forced into a brief shootout. During the exchange, Hazen's horse was spooked and threw its rider. The delay allowed the bandits to gain cover in the hills.

"They ain't nothin' but deputized farmers," Logan spits. "We hit Hazen and they'll wet themselves."

Both Curry and Logan were known killers already. Their hands were covered in death. But Wyoming balked at the suggestion. Curry did not. Not wanting to be known as a coward, Wyoming rode out with the assassins and broke the posse in half. Logan got a bead on Hazen, who no longer had a horse, and gut-shot him. He died in the dirt and dust of their galloping horses.

Curry had them ride to Castle Creek, where they left the horses and waded downstream. It was a like a death march to

Wyoming. He had a long time to think about Hazen as they plodded all the way to the Tisdale Mountains on foot. He didn't see Butch again until weeks later. After a prolonged stay at Hole-in-the-Wall, Wyoming rode silently down through Horsethief Canyon to Brown's Hole, hating Logan the entire way.

When the heat from the Wilcox robbery finally died away, most of the gang members took jobs on a ranch outside Alma, New Mexico. It was a quiet season, and even though the rancher knew who they were, he left them alone. Besides, it was to his advantage having the Wild Bunch on his payroll. Their presence was a significant deterrent to rival rustlers in the area.

Partway through the summer, Butch heard that Buffalo Bill's Wild West and Congress of Rough Riders would be making a stop across the border in Texas. Intrigued by reports of the show's long-standing success, he convinced Wyoming and Sundance to make the trip with him to see it. Wyoming was already familiar with the story of William Frederick Cody. Or at least E.Z.C. Judson's version of the legend. He had leafed through numerous dime-store comics detailing the frontiersman's adventures.

He had been a rider for the Pony Express at the tender age of fourteen, and a cavalry officer with the Union army in Kansas. But of course, he was most famous for his later exploits with the Fifth Cavalry in Wyoming's Indian Wars. It was said that he scalped a Cheyenne warrior in single combat. He was also given a Congressional Medal of Honor for his work as a scout.

But the moniker of Buffalo Bill came from his days immediately following the Civil War, when he took a job providing meat for the Kansas Pacific Railway workers. There it was reported that he killed over four thousand buffalo with the same number of bullets.

Wyoming was just as excited to meet the legendary marksman

as Butch. And, of course, Sundance was as excited as he ever got. Meaning that he was no better than a wet blanket. But once in Alma, Wyoming had to admit that he was disappointed with the display. With the exception of Little Sure Shot, Annie Oakley, he knew a dozen guys who could perform the same tricks. But if Wyoming was left unimpressed, Butch was positively morose.

"They're makin' fun of us, Harry," he said to Sundance as they were leaving. "They're turnin' us inta a joke." The men walked back to their hotel in silence following those remarks, until Butch stopped them in the middle of the street. He looked back and forth between Wyoming and Sundance, studying them for a moment.

"I'm damn glad that I weren't around in the days ole Sittin' Bull was with 'em. Yes, sirs. I'd of been some sad to see that."

Wyoming wasn't sure what upset Butch so much at first. But it was shortly after this trip that rumours of Cassidy's reform began to circulate. Perhaps they all should have moved on then.

South of Roundup the men steal fresh horses. It has been more than a week since any of them have bathed or shaved, but they do not go into town. Wyoming has the itchings of his first beard, but Harvey and Ben look like bushmen. Birds could nest in their whiskers.

Wyoming asks, "Why ain't we turned around yet? How far north do you intend to go?"

"Landusky," Harvey replies.

"Shit," says the boy.

Logan is a man to be feared, for sure. Wyoming knows this much to be true. So he can't fault the Tall Texan for falling into line. In all the time he's known the murderer, Wyoming has learned that the man has little fear and fewer scruples. In fact, the only thing at which the bandit is known to balk is the Indian.

Walking out of a saloon in Deadwood, he'd come face to face with a band of "wild" Lakota. Wild, because they had refused the government's order to turn themselves over to the reservation. As such, most of the town's citizenry was giving the band a wide berth. Rumour had it they were part of a renegade party who were rattling the gold prospectors in the Black Hills, and that they were in Deadwood for shells.

Logan was young and drunk, living large as a member of Black Jack Ketchum's gang. But the way Matt Warner told it to Wyoming, you never saw a man turn so pale, so quickly. When Warner asked him why the Indians upset him so much, he only grumbled, "I'm not partial to losing my hair just yet."

But Wyoming once heard another explanation from Butch. Apparently, Logan was one quarter Cheyenne himself—a story supported by his dark hair and complexion, if not his features. And years later, while drinking with Butch in Powder Springs, he brought the subject up of his own accord.

"It's like they can read my thoughts. Like they know I'm some kinda half-breed turncoat."

But whatever the reason, it was certainly an anomaly. And Wyoming is not expecting any renegade Lakotas to come to his aid.

Harvey Logan arrived in the outlaw world by accident of destiny. His role in a Colorado saloon brawl sent him into hiding at the infamous outlaw headquarters of Hole-in-the-Wall. He borrowed his name from the bandit Flat-Nosed Curry, and added to that his own nickname of Kid—a moniker he garnered while ranching in Texas. Up until this point in his life, Kid Curry was a legitimate rancher and cowhand. He owned his own place in Fergus County, Montana. But he had a bad temper that exploded two days after Christmas in 1894—the night he killed Pike Landusky.

After that, he took up with the Black Jack Ketchum Gang and began robbing trains. Logan was infamous for his gun battles with lawmen, and his numerous narrow escapes. Killing came to him naturally. And once he opened the floodgates, there was no turning back.

They come across a cabin on the outskirts of Landusky just after dark. It is a solid log home, surrounded by several outbuildings. The yard is fenced in. All day, Logan has been whistling and humming. He is positively playful as they draw near. Wyoming has been trying all day, without success, to convince Kilpatrick to leave with him and forget the money. Now, Harvey has them abandon their horses and approach the cabin on foot. The home is dark, but the yard is lit by the light of the waxing moon. The three crouch by the fenceline.

"Oh, Mr. Winters!" Harvey sings. "Oh, Jimmy Winters!"

Wyoming steals a look at Kilpatrick, who is biting down on his lower lip.

"Mr. Winters, your cows is loose in the fields and there's rustlers about, altering your brand and stealing your unmarked mavericks."

The three men hide in the shadows. After a brief delay, some-one strikes a light in the house. A few moments later, the front door swings open and a short middle-aged man with a small pot-belly and bandy legs steps out. He holds the lantern high with his left hand. In his right, he trains a fowling piece on the night.

"Who's out there?"

The puddle of light dropped by the lantern casts an awful shadow over the man's face. He looks like something called up from the dead to lead Wyoming into Hell.

"I said who's there?"

"Just us ghosts," Harvey teases him.

Ben lets a laugh escape from his nose. But when Wyoming looks at him, he is rubbing both legs with his hands, and rocking back and forth on the balls of his feet nervously.

"Who is that? Stand up, so's I can see ya."

To Wyoming's amazement, Logan stands. Draws himself up to full height.

"You." The word barks like a gunshot.

Even in the dark, the recognition is immediate. The man's face twists in disdain. Too late, Wyoming sees Logan's pistol flash in the night. The bullet hits the man just below the nose, and his mouth disappears in a terrible spray of black blood and bits of bone.

Wyoming is too stunned to move. He knows now that there is no girl. Harvey has been planning this man's death since they left the Bearpaw Mountains and returned north. Logan steps into the yard and stoops over the dead body of rancher Jim Winters. A small kerosene fire burns in the dirt where the lantern lies smashed. Satisfied, Logan stands and kicks at it as he moves toward the porch.

"See to that mess, will ya, boys," he says, cool as river water.

The thing about riding with Butch was that he lived up to his reputation. Whether or not he had a code of conduct before he joined the Outlaw Trail, or whether he invented one based on the stories of his exploits in the paper, did not matter to Wyoming. What mattered was that he was different from the others.

Old Matt Warner told Wyoming about the time Butch was caught for stealing a small bunch of horses from a rancher by the name of Jim Kittleman. He was young and inexperienced. Kittleman trailed the thief himself and then had a warrant drawn up for the outlaw's arrest. Two officers carried out the warrant and confiscated the horses. Cassidy gave himself up willingly and was reported to have cooperated with the officers in every way. As they transported him to the county seat, Butch whistled snatches of old tunes and commented on the quality of the day.

It was hot and the officers elected to make camp in the shade for lunch. The two men, lulled by Cassidy's affable personality, paid little attention to their prisoner as they made preparations for a meal. While one moved off in search of water, Butch gave the other, who was settled on his haunches by the cooking fire, a quick shove with his boot. The man rolled forward, concentrating on avoiding the flames. At the same time Butch sprang to life and lifted the officer's gun. The returning lawman raised his hands in surrender when he noticed Butch already had a bead on him. Cassidy unfastened his manacles and rode off with the stolen horses, plus two.

For most men, this might have been the end of the story. But Butch realized during his escape that he had neglected to leave the men a canteen. On foot in the middle of the Utah desert, without water, they would most assuredly have died. Understanding this, Butch turned back.

The three men shared a smoke after Butch had apologized for the oversight. And when he left the second time everyone concerned felt much better about the whole affair. Only Butch was sure to keep the ponies.

It was difficult to separate myth from the man in a time of oral history and unreliable narrators, but Wyoming had ridden with Butch for almost three years. He knew that he could believe the myths.

It turns out Ben has not lied about the girl. There had been a girl at one point—Elfie Landusky, daughter of Pike Landusky, town founder. But that had been years ago. Logan shot Landusky dead in a local saloon after he'd been humiliated by a false assault charge against the man's daughter. Pike Landusky had the charge trumped up after he beat Elfie himself in a fit of rage. She was pregnant at the time, and lost the child. Logan skipped town before the trial and returned only one time after that.

Ben has Winters by the feet.

"Winters had been spying on him. Hoping to cash in on the reward, I guess."

"So Harvey came to kill him?"

"Yep. Only Winters weren't alone."

"What happened?"

"Winters shot Johnnie Logan—Harvey's kid brother. Harvey and Lonny managed to escape."

"So this is payback," says Wyoming, indicating the ruined head lolling in front of him.

"It's been a long time coming."

"You realize that we're murderers now, Ben? We might as well of pulled the trigger ourselfs."

Kilpatrick cannot look him in the eye. Instead, he ignores the boy and moves backward across the yard, half dragging the dead rancher between them. Wyoming halts the man's progression by restraining the body. Kilpatrick drops the man's feet and stands up. His lanky form throws a long shadow over the boy.

"What are you doin'?"

"Listen, Ben. You can't like this anymore'n I do. What say we take the money and head south, like was planned."

"How do you propose we do that? You gonna shoot Kid Curry?"

"What say we get that bastard good and liquored up tonight. When he passes out, we grab the sack and release his horse. By the time he comes to, we'll be halfway to the Powder River."

The Texan's eyes shift back and forth.

"Can't do it, kid. He'd hunt us down like dogs."

He stoops to pick up the body once more. When they reach the salt house, Kilpatrick kicks open the door and pulls the dead man over the threshold. The room is cool and damp. Several inches of water cover the dugout floor. Wyoming stares down at the shattered head, half submerged among jars of jam and pickled beets. It is the saddest sight he has ever seen.

That night the boy dreams. He is back among the shorthorns south of the Gillette. He is fifteen. His father is dead, and the dirt farm he grew up on is a state away and slowly returning to earth. Buffalo grass knocks at the door. It is a cold spring morning after rain. A grey day split open by sun. He can hear the mavericks kicking and bawling as the cowboys pull them out of the wild and difficult areas. They drive toward the blue smoke of their cottonwood fires on the north shore of the Belle Fourche River. The sun is covered in dust.

He watches as the ropers, like himself, move in and heel the calves by the hind legs with lightning precision. The wrestlers arrive in pairs, pressing their weight into the warm flanks of the animal. An older hand pulls a brand from the fire. Those were happy days among the tough men, under the big bowl of sky. An idyllic time, it seems to him now, although he can't say that he regrets his run with Butch.

He is a better man for having met him. This much he knows. Only he feels that he has overstayed his welcome. And maybe Butch has too. The world is rocketing forward without them. It's a new century now and somehow it has left them behind. He is not sure that the future has room for him or the likes of Butch— cowboys and outlaws. He certainly can't think of any success stories. The ones who haven't ended up in jail or dead usually work themselves useless. Or worse, they have ended up in some travelling freak show in a parody of western romance.

What Wyoming needs is a plan. He needs a way out.

When he wakes, it is still night. Flashes of sheet lightning spark off in the distance, but no thunder. Kilpatrick is next to him on the floor. When he is certain of the man's rhythmic breathing, the boy rises and moves through the lifeless rooms of the cabin. Harvey is asleep in Winters's bed. An empty bottle of whiskey lies among the sheets. The sack of unmarked banknotes is loose on the floor. Harvey snores, sprawled across the sheets like a dog.

He could shoot him now, he thinks. He has never hated anyone as he does Logan. The air is close and warm in the room. Quietly, he removes the bag from the floor and places it over his shoulder. He takes the revolver from its holster under his arm. He leans in close, so he can smell the man's sour breath. The muzzle of his pistol is almost inside Logan's ear. The hammer makes a soft click as he pulls it back, but in the still of the cabin, it sounds like an explosion. Harvey snores on, oblivious. The gun is a stone in his hand.

"Bang," he whispers close to the murderer's face before creeping backward out of the room and into the night.

By morning, Wyoming has gained the Milk River west of Wagner. Logan is right about one thing. No one would suspect him to be back so close to the scene of the crime. He has given up on his quest for Hole-in-the-Wall. Lefors will be waiting for him there, and if not—it will be the first place Logan seeks him out. Sirango's men will be well south into Utah by now. Close on the heels of Butch and Sundance. They'll tear up Robber's Roost, send agents into Nevada, Arizona. They'll scour New Mexico and end up empty-handed in Texas. He knows that Butch is leaving the country, and that he is on his own. He can feel it in his gut.

It has been a blistering summer in Montana and already the plain is a blast furnace. He has been riding now for almost three weeks, all told. His clothes are soiled and the stench of his own body is almost unbearable. An acrid smell like fermented onions. His horse carries him over the slow-moving river at the same ford the Wild Bunch used to escape earlier in the month. Tired and wet, he hobbles the horse amongst a stand of aspen and cottonwood on the other side of the bank. This way, he will not be visible should someone happen along the road on the south side of the river. He hangs his clothes in the branches of a nearby tree and stretches out in the shade. He is hungry but too beat to search for anything. He stays there most of the afternoon to recuperate his strength, then remounts his horse and rides west between the railway and the river.

Sundance told him once that the river would take him across the border into Canada. Sundance spent two years in Calgary at a place called the Bar U ranch. It is there that Wyoming is determined to go now. He rides through the burnt grassland owned by the railroad, coming so close to the tracks at some points he can watch the trains passing between Havre and Wagner. Now and again, the road and the rail line overlap and he is forced into hiding among bullrushes and larkspur until the traffic has passed. Once a stagecoach passes within spitting distance. The guards carry Spencer repeaters perched on their hips like lances.

It takes him two days to travel the short distance to Havre like this. By then he is so hungry and exhausted, he is on the verge of collapse. He has no choice but to leave the river and enter the town.

Wyoming tethers the horse in a sheltered hollow just back from the river and stows the bag of useless money nearby. He cannot risk having the animal spotted and he has nothing with which to alter the brand. He washes himself as best as he can, but his clothes remain filthy. Covered in five hundred miles of dust.

When night falls he sneaks into town and scavenges whatever he can find. He breaks into the general store—shattering a window to the pantry—and makes off with a sack of potatoes and as many tins of beans as he can carry. For the first time in days, he has what resembles a proper meal, but he does not risk a fire so close to the road. As he cleans out a second tin of beans and bites into the raw flesh of an uncooked potato, Wyoming realizes what a pitiful state he is in. His hair is matted and oily. A patchwork of dirty blond whiskers covers his chin. His nails are broken and split. Black soil has worked its way into the fibre of his skin, so that his body is a map of dark rivers and shoals.

He cannot continue this way. Calgary is still several days' north, and even longer if he must camp and hide out along the way. There is a sack full of money in his possession and yet it is useless without a signature. If it were only a matter of stealing a pen, but he can't even read, much less write. Logan's words have become a prophecy.

Then it comes to him. The first stirring of an idea. And then he finds himself laughing aloud in the middle of a salt marsh with only a horse to hear him.

Butch Cassidy invented the daylight bank robbery to pay for a friend's legal fees. Matt Warner was on trial in Salt Lake City. Butch Cassidy, Elzy Lay, and Joe Meeks had promised to foot the lawyer's bill. To do that, they targetted the Montpellier bank in Idaho. The three men drove their horses into town and tied them to a hitchpost outside the local saloon. All three had a drink, and then Cassidy took a walk past the bank in order to note the positions of the cashiers. Back at the saloon, he described his simple plan to Lay and Meeks.

Just before closing, one of the cashiers stepped outside for some fresh air. Butch and Elzy moved in quickly with their guns beneath their coats. The cashier led the armed men inside and asked the other tellers to come out. Elzy had them face the wall while Butch scooped out the drawers. The whole operation was over in minutes. Meeks was across the street with all three horses.

One of the cashiers sounded the alarm almost immediately following Butch's exit, but it was some time before a posse could be assembled. The outlaws changed horses at a preordained drop and led the lawmen on a twelve-day chase. The posse returned empty-handed. Butch made away with six thousand one hundred and sixty-five dollars in banknotes, and another thousand in gold.

This is why the outlaws loved him, and the lawmen despised him. When the old ways wouldn't do, he invented new ones.

Wyoming rides the horse into town just after 9:00 a.m. The shops have only just begun to stir with life. His appalling appearance draws the attention of a few pedestrians. But for the most part, they are used to seeing cowhands off the range for a drink, and they do not molest him.

He has gone over the plan again and again—but in the end, these things boil down to a rather time-honoured routine. Wyoming ties the bay to a hitch-post behind the Havre Community Bank—in similar fashion to the heist at Montpellier—and strolls around to the front of the building, where he steps into the dim interior as though he owns the place. Swaggering over the floor like a tiny God.

It is not the first bank Wyoming has had a hand in robbing. But it is the first job he has ever done solo. And without a yegg-man to scout things out, there are any number of variables that can go wrong.

A single teller mans the lone wicket. Before him is the bank's only customer—an elderly woman in her Sunday bonnet. Wyoming steps up and moves her gently aside. He withdraws the Remington from its hiding place and sticks it through the wicket into the round fat face of the teller.

"Give me everything in the cashbox, if you please. This is a holdup."

The plump little teller stares out at him with small eyes lost in the fat of his cheeks.

"Son, we've only just opened for business. There's nothing but a few dollars in the float."

"That's all I need. Now if you please," he repeats, wagging the pistol.

"Excuse me, but I believe I was here first," squawks the elderly woman in the bonnet.

"I beg your pardon, ma'am?"

"That's Missus Whitby. You'll have to speak up. She can't hear so good."

"Is she blind too?"

Wyoming waves the revolver in front of the little woman and yells, "This is a holdup, ma'am!"

Just then, the woman raises her purse and smashes it down on the side of Wyoming's head. The blow lands on his temple and leaves his ears ringing.

"You're not taking my money. You little hooligan!" The woman hauls back for another attack. Wyoming just manages to escape.

"Jesus, missus. I don't want yer money. I want his," Wyoming says, waving the gun in the teller's direction.

"What did you say?"

"Speak up, son. I told you she's—"

"I know, I know. She don't hear so good."

"I hear just fine," she bellows and moves in again, brandishing the purse.

"Ma'am, don't make me shoot you," he yells.

"You wouldn't dare," gasps the teller.

"Shut up and give me that cashbox, for crissakes."

"What's going on here?" says a farmer just inside the door.

"It's a holdup," answers the teller, as Wyoming is otherwise indisposed.

"By whom?"

"Me, you eejit. Who else? Put your hands above your head."
But the entire time he is speaking, the elderly woman batters him
relentlessly with her purse.

"Are you okay?" asks the teller after a particularly well-aimed
kick surprises the boy.

"Lord almighty. Just give me the cash!"

"I don't think that I can do that."

"Why not?"

"I don't believe that you'll shoot me."

Wyoming stops in the centre of the room after dancing away
from Missus Whitby. "You don't believe that I'll shoot you?"

The teller shakes his head. Wyoming looks to the farmer, who
has obediently raised his hands. "You believe I'll shoot you,
right?"

The farmer pauses a moment and shakes his head in response.

"Then why do you have yer hands up?"

The farmer shrugs and lowers his arms.

"No! Put them back up. Jesus."

Wyoming catches the approach of a fourth body in the corner
of his eye at the same moment that he ducks to avoid another blow
from the woman's purse. She is tiring now. But as he moves to the
window for a closer look, Wyoming can see that the newcomer is
the sheriff. The star displayed proudly on his pigeon chest.

"Ah, Jesus."

Turning to the wicket he seizes the pen and the bottle of ink
beside it, before slipping out the front door and down the steps.
He tips his hat politely to the sheriff, who nods in return.

The town is a hornet's nest that has just been struck with a stick.
Wyoming breaks his way through the back door of a two-storey
hotel just down the street. He knows immediately from the smell
of camphor that he has entered a brothel. Most of the women are

gathered on the verandah outside the front door, languishing in the early day heat, observing the confusion of the townspeople. The news of a failed robbery has just reached them, and already they are clucking like hens.

Wyoming flies up the back steps two at a time and makes his way down the upstairs hallway. He enters an open door at the front of the building and finds himself in the room of a young lady. The walls are papered in a red velvet motif. The curtains are chintz. The wardrobe is open and draped with a plethora of dresses and undergarments he does not even recognize. On the dressing table sit a number of lotions and potions of varying scents. If he did not know better, he might think himself in the shop of an apothecary. Out the front window, he watches as the posse assembles down the street. He can hear voices on the stairwell now. With no other options, he squeezes himself beneath the unmade bed.

It is a long day, and an even longer night. The bed bucks and twists. Its rusted springs wail and screech. Threatening to give way altogether. There is more traffic in that room than the local train depot a few blocks north. Cowboys and farmhands. Gamblers and gunslingers. Small-town officials and local politicians. All of them there for the same reason. Driven by the same ancient urge. But finally, in the wee hours before dawn, the house grows quiet and once again Wyoming can measure the steady breath of the bed's last occupant. Much deserving of her rest, as only he would know.

Wyoming creeps out from the safe haven of the young woman's bed into the thick air of the room. As he re-establishes his bearings, he notices the small pile of coinage and bills on the corner of the nightstand. The day is not a total loss.

He takes only one note. Enough for his purposes. It almost

breaks his heart to have to pinch her hard-earned money, but without a signature to copy, he does not have a chance of ever using the thirty thousand dollars lying beneath a tree just outside town.

In the last moment before he turns to exit the room, Wyoming freezes. Trapped in the pool of the woman's dark eyes. She does not speak. Does not cry out to give him away. And although he cannot be sure, there appears to be the hint of a smile curled on her lips. What the boy cannot know is how he appears to her in the dark of the room with a pale light bleeding in from the transom to the hall. He cannot know that she has been dreaming of a visitation like this since she was a child. And so, when Wyoming raises a finger on the tip of his dry lips—supplicating for silence—the young woman sees an angel offering comfort in the dead of another black night.

He slips down the steps, through the parlour and quietly out the front door. He stretches the atrophied muscles of his ill-used limbs, then looks up and down the deserted street. Thinking perhaps if he is lucky. But the old bay mare has disappeared. Resigned to his new fate, Wyoming sets off down the road he came in. On foot.

Milk River

VECCHA KNOWS WITHOUT LOOKING THAT THEY ARE OUTSIDE THE cabin. Some will have been waiting since dawn, having left their homesteads south of Foremost in the dark to arrive first. But always they are outdone by the seekers from Coutts and Milk River—fewer in number, but closer in distance. She lifts the long cotton-coloured hair from her shoulders and ties it in place on the top of her head. Her white skin looks darker in the cracked mirror fastened to the washstand. She refers to them all as seekers, regardless of their origins. For that is what they are. Seekers and searchers. She moves through the curtain that separates the room, pulling it closed behind her to hide the unmade bed.

In the kitchen, she breaks kindling into the clay stove that squats in the corner like a Buddha. She does not rush. When the fire is set, she pours water into a kettle from the earthen jug. She lays a cloth upon the table, and a set of cups upon the cloth. The china is so fine, a pure light might pass through it. With an old twig broom, she sweeps dust from the loose floorboards. The door waits for her hand to set it free.

63

Over the threshold Veccha stares into the yard, which is a silent garden. The blue sky spills in around her and runs in search of texture. For a moment, she sees them stiff as statuary, until they turn. Blinking at the reflection of her white dress in the sun.

Every Sunday they arrive in search of answers. She pours them tea, which is carried by train to Lethbridge from cities in the east, and brought to her by pack horse. She speaks to them while they drink from the delicate cup. And holding it afterward in the palms of her two hands, she reads to them from the future. She is a clairvoyant. A tasseographer. This is what she does.

Veccha swirls the remaining liquid clockwise three times before turning it into the saucer below. When she brings it back to rest in her hands, the visions will come. Or they will not. The leaves are a gateway, a medium sprinkled in lines and various shapes. Tapering away from the rim to the future. Sometimes they are clear, and the seeker is lucky. Often the objects are blurred. The outcome uncertain. But there are other times when she has no need of the cup. Of the tea. Times when the seeker's face is enough. The future as clear as a dream.

She has ministered to the seekers for months and knows the muted passion in their faces well. They come to her resolute and grave. With questions about crops, the health of their children, relatives who do not return letters, sons gone north to the mines, sons gone east to the city. Sons in South Africa. In Stormberg. Magersfontein. Nicholson's Nek. And Paaderburg. Places burned on their tongues. The previously unimagined landscapes of the Boer War.

And so she reads to them from the leaves, and she soothes them with the balm of her words. She assuages their fears with hope at the bottom of a well. Or she cries with them. And they thank her. They pat her hands. They raise their broken fingers to the slope of her cheek, and they tell her that she is still a pretty girl. That there will be others before long. That they too can see into the future, and for her, it is bright. *It can not be otherwise,* they tell her, *for such a good girl.*

And she guides the women back to the only door in her cabin. Back to their husbands who kick stones by the river, but who look up nonetheless. And their eyes say, *Remember, I am not a believer. But what did you find?*

Helga Gustufson is a regular seeker. She comes for news of her sister every week. Without fail. Helga came to Canada with her husband only last year. But he is a drinker. If they cannot put forty acres under the plough, they will lose the land they were given. The government will repossess. Which would be fine for Helga. It is the first time since birth that she has been separated from her sister, who still lives in the hamlet of Punt.

"We used to ski every day in the winter once the chores were completed," she tells Veccha between sips from the hot cup. Once they are in her kitchen, there is no need to rush. Her home is the long-awaited letter they fear to open.

"And in the summer, we would watch the fishing boats unloading their catch in the harbour. Did you ever do that, Veccha? When you were a child?"

"I do not remember, Mrs. Gustufson. Are you through with your tea?"

And always, they look to the cup in their hands. Surprised almost that the moment has come so soon. Hesitant to give up their ignorance and yet yearning for knowledge. She smiles. Relinquishes her hold on the present, and passes the cup over the laundered weft of the tablecloth. A pool of spilt milk in the room.

Today is easy. There is almost no need to look. The patterns are simple. A flag and a boat. These she can deal with. But in the end, there is also a cross.

"What is it? What do you see?"
"Your sister," says Veccha. And the vision is clear.

The first Scandinavian immigrants arrived in Alberta from the Dakota Territory in 1882. They were Icelanders who settled near Red Deer. The Swedes soon followed. Then the Danes and the Finns. Eventually, Veccha's Norwegian countrymen were equally well represented. Scattered all over the Canadian territory like seeds.

They came for the cheap land. One hundred and sixty acres for ten dollars. All they had to do was build a house and put forty acres under the plough within three years. Some failed. The promised land proved almost untameable. Prairie fires and extreme drought in the summer. Insects enough to drive them mad. And in the winter, most tied a lifeline between the barn and their tiny sod homesteads, lest they be lost in the terror of a snow squall. Aside from the grain they tried to grow in the fields, standard fare consisted of rabbits, prairie dogs, and fowl.

But many toughed it out as well. The Scandinavians, in spite of their haphazard settlement, grew together in communities. They built rural schools before they constructed churches. The families gathered around the pot-bellied stoves of their sod huts, while the men read aloud. Women spun and knit wool. And eventually their earthen homes were returned to the land in exchange for cut timber cabins.

When work on her father's property was completed, Veccha's brothers took advantage of another incentive and purchased adjoining quarters for three dollars. They were shrewd men with broad shoulders. Her father had been a schoolmaster in Egersund. His neighbours were fishermen. And yet, they could all claim to be successful farmers in the new world. That was all that mattered here anyway.

Veccha's Norway was a place of mystery and folklore even at the end of the nineteenth century. She was born in a small fishing village called Egersund. Surrounded by the natural disaster of avalanches, mountain slides, floods, ocean storms, and winters paralleled only in her new home of Canada, the average rural Norwegian still believed in the supernatural. They turned to fairy tales to explain the world around them. In a land so precarious and sublime, it is not difficult to believe in gods and heroes. In lake giants and trolls.

And of course, there were people like Veccha's mother, and like Veccha. One could deny the existence of a lake troll, but it would be more difficult to refute the magic of women like Veccha's mother. And if one could exist, then why not the other? So the people lived a simple life. A hard life. They made offerings to their gods and they told their stories around hearths once attended by the Vikings.

Veccha's father was a schoolmaster, but he was also a fisherman like most other men in her village. And so were her brothers. Those who were old enough to go to sea. But their world was disappearing. Each year more families left for the new world. For America. Left for the promise of more land. Sometimes entire villages would disappear in the space of a single season, the abandoned homes gaping like toothless faces staring out to sea. Veccha did not believe that she could ever leave that place. She did not accept that her father could. But she knew otherwise. And always this knowing without believing would be a part of her. Like the lake giants, the gods, and the trolls. Like the heroes she knew of, if only in her father's stories.

At night, Veccha dreams of her dead husband. Six months have passed and she still sees him as he appeared in life. He lumbers out of the field where he has been studying three-thousand-year-old petroglyphs along the coulee wall. From his shoulders hang two massive arms like hips of beef. He holds a stack of papers to his chest. The wind rifles through them as he enters the yard, head down, mumbling, and leaning into each step. He has mastered this. The art of incongruity. No matter what the situation, he is able to appear out of place. The path at his feet is beaten smooth by his passage.

"There's more to the story," he tells her. "There are more writings on the north wall wasted by time."

His eyes look down at her like fossilized stone. She touches his arm.

"Tell me."

"I've found the remains of a medicine wheel, Veccha."

"Yes."

It is noon on the prairie. The air is almost incandescent. His eyes drift to the sky beyond her left shoulder and the papers gripped to his chest are released to the wind. A lifetime of work.

"I am buried a long way from here, Veccha. I should have listened to you. This is not how I imagined our life."

She takes his useless hands in hers. She turns them over and over. The calluses have disappeared. The palms are just as soft and fat as the day she met him at the train station in Foremost. He held the grant money from the Royal Geographical Society in his pocket like a key.

Two Bears arrives under the heel of afternoon sun. The last of the wagons is eclipsed by the buffalo grass of the high plateaux. It is always like this. Perhaps he sits in wait along the ridge, she thinks. But it is more likely that he senses their departure like a buckle of wind. His brothers are with him. Grey ghosts in the background, each one of them. He does not leave his roost on the dun-coloured stallion, but he does lean forward to address her. A sign of respect. His arrival is the bright spot in her day.

The staccato hum of his mother tongue draws her in like an old blanket.

"There are changes in the wind?" he says, turning it into a question. This deference to her is flattering, but it never ceases to shame her in some way. Her cheeks flush under the scrutiny of his pale eyes.

"Yes. I feel it too." Her fat tongue struggles around the foreign vowels.

"Did you dream last night?"

"No."

"This is bad." No question this time. "There is a white man on the prairie. You will be careful?"

"Yes. Thank you, Two Bears. There are always men now."

"No. He is not like the others?" The questioning tone has returned to confuse her. Veccha withdraws her eyes from his gaze. Of course she dreamed, but not of this. It is not a lie really. It is the same dream that she always has.

"I do not know."

Now Two Bears is confused. He looks away to the south, across the coulee bottom.

"You will dream tonight."

"Perhaps," Veccha says in Norwegian. Two Bears repeats the word, nodding with the assurance of this newfound wisdom. This pebble she has offered him.

Two Bears was there from the beginning. Robert scribbling madly. Capturing thoughts and observations. So involved in his work that he did not notice the silent arrival. Became aware of the other man's presence through the hairs on his neck. When he turned from the wall, expecting to find Veccha, he imagined the Indian was an anthropomorphism of stone. The carving blossomed to real. Fear came later, he told her after the meeting. He had never seen a North American native before. He understood they were tamed. But there by the wall, boxed in by the man and his brothers, Robert thought he might die.

Of course this was not the case. The man asked him a question, but they had no language between them. Robert showed him the book—the pencil he used to reproduce the stone art. After that, the Indian returned again and again. Having little to do with Veccha at first. But her penchant for language—her facility with speech—gradually drew him into her sphere.

While Robert scribbled down words—gathered vocabulary and conjugated the verbs—Veccha grew into the Algonquian tongue like a child. And she became, for a time, their translator. The interpreter of questions and answers.

It was not until Robert left for South Africa that Two Bears began to call her the shaman.

Veccha refused to see Robert off at the train station in Foremost. She refused to say goodbye. He stooped under the low ceiling of their sod hut and tried to tell her that he would be back before Christmas. He had written her brothers and they would take her in if she needed them. There was no other choice, he said. They needed the money. But already he was dead to her—so clear was his fate. More palpable than the lines on his palm.

The train would take him to Manitoba, where he would enlist with the Winnipeg Rifles. From there, he would be ferried to Quebec for training.

"The war might be over by then," he laughed. "And I shan't have fired a shot."

She tries now to imagine how he must have looked among all those fresh and eager faces. Those turgid youthful bodies already marked with death. He would have appeared like an old man to them, she suspects. A dishevelled professor in wire-rim spectacles.

Would they have laughed at him? Or might they have turned to him for assurance? Fatherly advice? Surely not in those heady times of pipe bands and parades. Celebrations at every whistle stop holding up the train. No. He would have passed unnoticed and anonymous. It wouldn't be until they saw him in uniform that they would even know he was one of them.

And then, maybe they would have whispered. But not when they arrived in poor Cape Town. Not once they were in the sands of De Aar. And certainly not during the horrors of Paardeburg and "Pom Pom Tuesday." But by then, Robert would have been unable to comfort them. He would be gone.

Veccha is cold moving water. On the prairie this is wrong. Incompatible. It is the way she has always been. A misfit in every situation. Someone outside, peering through stone. She is aware of the classical myths. Her mother told her everything about Cassandra and the curse. The curse she herself would come to know like every other woman in her mother's family. The curse like a needle sliding violent through generations. Knitting the women together. Tossing links into the chaos of the world.

Others have called it *the gift*. Because they cannot know. Cannot possibly understand what it is like to have the random curiosity of a life stripped away like skin in raw patches of hurt. A salve does not exist for this. No balm. They have come to her for years now. Ever since her mother died. Like a passing of the torch. But the villagers always knew she had it. The gift-curse of her ancestors, like a slow clock ticking in her blood. It was in the way they stared at her when she passed on her way to school. The way teachers would always turn to her when no other child knew the answer.

How could they ever understand that it did not work this way? That it was as unlike a conjuring as falling off a cliff. That it was, in fact, a sinking. Always a slow pull into the rivers of time.

Robert had saved her from all this, or so she thought. She had been dreaming him since childhood. The man from far away. The rescuer, she called him. But her own clairvoyance had failed even in this. For she was, in the end, mistaken. Robert had moved her away, indeed. But only a carriage ride. Of course his English horse sense and his love of all things scientific had forbade the admittance of her seekers for a time. But his death allowed them back into her life like sluice gates parting for the sea. And so she became the woman she was before, the woman who looked into pale wanting faces, lonely as cattle and just as needy. Only now, she needs them too.

She is cold moving water on the prairie. What does she know about broken fences? About fields gone fallow? The circle is complete. She has become a parasite that slowly eats her host. She has always been a stoic. It is part of what she does. Of what she is. But her dreams led her to believe in something more. Who else does she deceive with signals and signs?

The truth is Veccha is slowly letting go of the homestead. Freeing her will from its management. The rickety windmill squeaks on without her acknowledgement. Fences remain unmended. And often the cow must low before she will tend to its milking. She keeps a kitchen garden but only because she must eat. Robert's money is gone. All that remains are half-empty stores of flour and beans. Coffee and tea. Her brothers sent meat from a slaughtered pig packed in salt. She does only the chores necessary to her survival. She was not meant for this life. Not because she is not tough enough, but because it was not meant to be.

She is waiting, she realizes, for something to happen. The next vision. Each day she spends less and less time with the running of Robert's house, and more and more time with the books he has unwittingly bequeathed her. She feeds herself with knowledge. Stories about cretaceous inland seas, pre-glacial river systems, moraines, deltas, esker-kame complexes, and palaeolithic Stone Age cultures. Robert's journals are now open to her as well.

Australia. Ayers Rock and aboriginal magic. These are the things she could never get from him. The passion behind the science. And still the mystery of life is not evident. Phrases hidden between lines. The hurried scrawl of thought, or the painstaking penmanship of careful reflection. Clues to something greater.

In the back of her mind, she is aware of winter's slow approach. Her need to leave this place. But she cannot return to her father and her brothers—although they would have her without a thought. It is the matter-of-fact acceptance of her eventual return that keeps her away. For the moment, Veccha exists in a dream world. A hiatus in the rush of life. She has her seekers. And Two Bears. Her books and the ever-present wall.

The longer the dream drags on, the less disposed she is to wake from it. Reality will spill in soon enough, she thinks. The violence of the too-bright world. Its constant threat at the door. Knocking.

Veccha remembers Oslo like a nightmare. A world of quarried stone. Boxes of time chiselled and mislaid. Chaos. Her father thought it the heart of the civilized world. He took her from building to building. Naming each architect. Explaining the history. They were only there a couple of days. Awaiting the boat that would ferry them to America. To her father's brother in North Dakota. It was the only time her father took such a personal interest in her education. Allowing her brothers to run wild on the docks as he dragged her to all the appropriate museums. She had never seen such things. So many people. So many futures colliding like atoms.

When he showed her the library in the university where he studied as a youth, she was smothered by the weight of volumes. The attempt to capture the past. She had always felt that her father was distant, that perhaps he feared her as the others did.

But during those few days of Norwegian spring, he was a changed man. He had something to give her. Maybe he felt that he had to, as he was removing them all from their home. She never asked him. And he was never so giving again.

He was solemn on the ship to America. And lost in the streets of New York. When they arrived in the hard lands of Dakota, he was already a different man.

Handbills and cheap land eventually brought them further north. Other Norwegians were settling in Claresholm and Fore-most. He purchased one hundred sixty acres for ten dollars. Her father and her three brothers nearly killed themselves with work in the first year. But they were not born to failure, as Veccha already knew. And then Robert arrived like a salesman.

She did not trust the dark in the first few weeks following Robert's disappearance. The black empty bowl of night seemed a betrayal. This was not the life she had foreseen as a child. But gradually, as one gets used to new rooms, she found the darkness homely. And she always knew that he was out there, along the coulee ridge, perhaps. Two Bears, her ancient knight.

And there is never silence on the prairie. Every night is full of song. The soprano chirp of a leopard frog. The cymbal crash of a diving muskrat. Or the alto snatch of bobcat on the lope. These were her comforts. These, and a light to read by.

The books that Robert left her were like swing doors into lost worlds. She grew a new vocabulary: Cenozoic, Cretaceous, Pre-cambrian. And with it the world began to appear to her in layers. Plates that she might shift and step through into time. She gleaned new meaning in the land. But her understanding only made things more mysterious. Two Bears's myths seemed like gospel. In the end, what she longed for were conflicting stories. It was her only chance at chaos.

Wyoming's stomach is a knotted rope. The high plain drags on hollow and empty. He has not eaten in two days. Havre's raw potato and beans seem more like a feast now. The hunger is making him dizzy. On the horizon, he thinks he sees a rider. But when he blinks and looks harder, whatever he saw is gone. The night before he tried in vain to copy the signature. Scratch out a facsimile. He wasted note after note. Dirtied his fingers. Stained the front of his shirt. And at last, in frustration, tossed the vile liquid into the flames of his fire. Snapped the pen in two. His failure to copy the signature sufficiently means nothing now. Currency is useless in the desert. He tried shooting grouse earlier, but his ruined eyes failed him.

For two days he passes through country too rough for life. Antique hoodoos rise out of the earth to dwarf his passage. Granite pillars like sculptured portals. Ironstones dead at their doorsteps. He has no company but the wheeling gyre of a hawk on the hunt. And each sunset sets the air incarnadine. Yet he cannot help but see the raw beauty in a land that is slowly rubbing him out like the head of a pencil.

At the end of the second day his tongue is so fat with thirst it spills past his lips, which are horribly chapped. His body has begun to itch uncontrollably. He is in danger of flaying himself entirely, when the earth opens before him like a cracked nut, and spits up the scent of a river.

Wyoming slides and tumbles down the steep incline of the coulee wall in the failing light of day. But he cannot feel the scrapes and cuts and bruises blooming over his parched flesh. He can only think of water until he is on his knees in the stream, sinking his hands into the current. Bringing the water up to his mouth in waves before submerging his head entirely. Had it not been for the Havre posse, he would never have left the river's shore.

He must be in Canada now, he reasons, slowing his intake. Out of harm's way, at least momentarily. The Pinks care little for borders. And Logan even less.

Wyoming picks his way along the shoreline like a child, and things only get better.

He is almost upon the sod hut before it comes into focus. A fire is burning. Smoke rising in dark plumes from the chimney. Out back, there are several outbuildings. He can hear chickens in what must be the coop.

Wyoming approaches the target like a weasel. Almost laughing at the change in fortune. There are no windows on the north side of the hut. He anticipates a painless theft, but after the robbery in Havre he is determined not to be overconfident. The chickens are quiet, despite the intrusion. The eggs are still warm. His original plan was to take only them, but once confronted with the plump possibility of chicken, Wyoming cannot shake the thought of fresh meat.

All hell breaks loose as he grabs the first hen. Its fellow inmates join in. Flapping. Squawking. And crashing into the walls. Wyoming aims for the exit. But smacks his forehead on the low threshold. Sprawled and chickenless, he shakes his head in an effort to stop the ringing in his ears. Through the crack in the door, he can see a blurred figure rounding the hut.

"Christ," he curses aloud. Fumbling to his feet, Wyoming withdraws the pistol from beneath his arm. The sun is setting in the west, and the figure is no more than a silhouette. Wyoming crouches in the dark recess of the coop.

When the door slides back, he aims the long-barrelled Remington at the chest of the approaching shadow.

Veccha keeps the rifle loaded at all times. Fox come from miles around. Attracted by the irresistible scent of her chickens. She does not expect to find more than this as she slides the small gun under her arm and enters the gathering twilight of her yard.

She is not concerned until she notices the door of the coop

cracked open, swinging slightly on its hinges. Two Bears's warning plays like a record as she enters the warm hut. She is momentarily startled as her eyes light on the crouching figure in the corner. The elf-like boy squinting in the gloom. His sandy blond hair shoots off in all directions. Sprouting like bean plants from under his black sombrero cap. His features are small and pinched. And at first, his eyes are hard, the brow furrowed. But slowly, for no reason she can discern, the corners of his chapped mouth turn upward into a mischievous grin.

When he stands and reveals himself entirely, she is surprised to see that he is shorter than she is. He raises an arm to his cap. Perhaps to tip it in greeting. But all she can see is the pistol. Aimed now at the ceiling. The boy winks at Veccha, just before she shoots him.

The Man from Pinkerton

THE BODY OF CAMILLO HANKS LIES TWISTED AND SURROUNDED by the splintered remains of a straight-backed chair. The man from Pinkerton stands above it, surveying the wreckage with the cold dead eyes of a fish. A continent of fresh blood stretches tectonic across the dead man's sunken chest. The room is quiet but for the barkeeper who sweeps crushed glass from the floor in a mechanical fashion. He avoids the crumpled corpse of the outlaw and the water that melts from the boots of the lawman.

Mackenzie Webb peels himself away from the seeping prey. The gun is still warm in his hand. Outside, the rain plays a white racket on the tin verandah. The lawman carves himself a chunk of tobacco with a pocket knife. Already the town's sheriff scampers down the muddied street with deputies in tow. The rain falls in sheets around them. The wrinkled man stops a moment on the step and looks hard into Webb's glass eyes. With a barely discernable tick, the sheriff motions the two deputies into the saloon ahead of him. His eyes linger on Webb's stone face. His bearded mask. Webb does not follow the sheriff inside.

The man from Pinkerton listens to the muted sound of men speaking as it rises and falls above the noise of the rain. But he makes no effort to sift it for meaning. He rode into Fort Worth on the edge of this storm. It tracked him clear down from Nashville. When he first arrived on the front steps of this verandah, the rain fell in big round drops, exploding like fireworks above his head. Now it is a slower, steady sound. An eddying stream. Hunger sits in his stomach like a cool stone.

The saloon doors crack open and swing in the wake of the sheriff's return. Webb's mind contorts, bringing the grizzled old man into focus for the first time. His eyes are bright beads lost in the folds of his skin. A dusting of white whiskers litters his chin like beaten chafe.

"You done this?"

Webb chews his tobacco. Nods his ascent.

"You a lawman?"

"Pinkerton's," Webb offers. The killing has sated his senses. The instinctual thirst that drove him like flotsam on flood water has receded.

"You got some kinda warrant?"

Webb reaches into the depths of his oilskin with mud-streaked hands to retrieve the soiled identification papers. There is a passport alongside a dog-eared *Wanted* poster among them. Satisfied, the sheriff passes them back.

"That man Butch Cassidy?"

"Camillo Hanks."

The old man nods and turns to the rain.

"Witnesses say he drawed on you."

"That so?"

A silence passes between them like cards.

"Ain't like it to rain in July," the sheriff offers. The two stand like that a long while, just staring at the rain. As though there were some mystery to it. As though by staring they might figure it out.

The wind is driving it now. Under the eaves, washing the floor at their feet. Eventually Webb steps off the verandah without so much as a glance at the sheriff and sets off down the street in the direction of the wire office. His black body gathers darkness to it like a well-made coat.

Mackenzie Webb was born and raised in Jacksonville, Illinois. The only child of Jethro and Mary Webb. As a child he was quiet and inordinately shy, a quality his teachers mistook for stupidity. And to make matters worse, he seemed to grow at an accelerated speed, so that by the age of ten, he was already six feet tall and weighed almost two hundred pounds. His father was a grocer and a God-fearing Baptist, in that order. And like his son, he stood an imposing six foot six in his sock feet, and tipped the scales at three hundred and fifty pounds—a condition that may well have saved him from the ranks of the Union army.

Each Sunday Jethro Webb dragged the family out to the small Baptist church for instruction in sin. Mackenzie was often uncomfortably packaged into a stiff suit and collar several sizes too small, as the family coffers could hardly keep up with their son's ever-expanding girth. As such, his memories of that time have more to do with discomfort and restriction than the words of the saviour. As it was, the old man followed blindly those same words, or at least those that it behooved him to remember, and he believed wholeheartedly, as his own father had, that to spare the rod was to spoil the child. So it came to pass that upon returning from their Sunday outing, Mackenzie received his weekly beating, whether one was particularly warranted or not.

When the boy turned twelve, he was required to leave school and help out at the store. But because of his aversion to public contact, his job was restricted to inventory, stocking, and sweeping. To outsiders, the family must have appeared the very picture of modest success. And so it was with a great deal of consternation and befuddlement that the community discovered on the Sunday following his eighteenth birthday, Mackenzie turned on his father. The man was busy rolling up his sleeves, as he had every Sunday for years, and preparing to educate the boy in humility, when Mackenzie decided that he had had enough.

The two were evenly matched in height, if not weight, but years of pent-up anger gave the boy a decided edge. In the end, the two blew out the back wall of their main street store and landed in the dust. And as luck would have it, Mackenzie ended up on top. A local blacksmith and two strangers finally pulled the boy off. Mackenzie left home that night.

He managed to find a part-time job off-loading riverboats at Quincy for a while. It was easy work and the pay was better than what he received at home, but the Mississippi River was a tough place, and young Webb soon learned that being a big man made him a target for every hooligan out to make a name for himself. Fortunately for Webb, there was enough anger and frustration lurking beneath his placid looks to last two lifetimes. Enough, in fact, to harness. And so, not too long after he left the sanctity of his parents' home, Webb found himself a second job as a bare-knuckles, London Rules prizefighter. A career that suited his appetite for violence. And one that might have gone well for him, had he not had the misfortune to kill a promising young Cajun fresh out of Baton Rouge.

And at that time in America, there were only two places for murderers. Prison and the military. So when one door closed, another one opened. Webb was just gathering steam.

From that point onward, everything Webb did seemed a grooming for Pinkerton's frontier operations. His adult life was a training ground in the arts of depravation and death. For years he

subsisted in the badlands of Wyoming, eventually landing a post-
ing with the 3rd Cavalry out of Laramie, during the uneasy
spring of 1876. There he met Sheridan and admired him greatly.
But not so much as Crook, under whom he served for much of
that year. Eating horsemeat on the infamous mud march. He
sniffed out his subsequent killings in the disastrous Reynolds Fight
and met Crazy Horse in the Battle of Rosebud that same July. That
summer he lost the last fragile trappings of civilization, sleeping
under the big sky of Montana and tracking Sioux war parties like a
loosed hound in the Black Hills of the Dakota Territory.

He was a gruelling campaigner. On the march he moved
slowly. Purposefully. As though conserving energy. A storm cloud
drinking in electrical charge. And then he exploded onto the field
of battle like a dervish possessed, moving through bodies like a
thrown knife. Wearing down the sharp edges of the humanity he
fostered in youth.

In one fight he took a well-aimed shell in the belly. It knocked
him from the seat of his horse, flat on his back, among sagebrush
and thistle. The sabre still charged in his hand. He lay stunned by
the pain as the massacre broiled around him. But he changed
then. Channelled the pain in his belly. Listened to the world
through his pores.

A moment later he was carving through hordes of advancing
Sioux warriors. Unaware that his comrades had retreated.
Were routed. Only the world within the length of his sword
was important. He would master that much through the force
of his will. At the base of his skull, the medulla took over.
Eking a primal drive others strive to suppress. It was a revelation. A calling.

And the cavalry lauded him. Dressed him in medals. Cultured
him like a pearl. It made ample use of his instinct for death in
those difficult times. But under the glowering grins of his leaders
lurked a fear no less primal than Webb's urge to kill. They feared
the end of war. They feared Webb at their dinner parties. Webb

with their wives. They discussed his handling over brandy and cigars. And they all agreed. He was not one of them.

Tracking Camillo Hanks to Fort Worth is an exercise in determination rather than intelligent detective work. Webb admits that freely. Hanks is no Butch Cassidy. Sly by less than half. But more importantly, the Wild Bunch underling does not have the same reputation, nor does he have the necessary friends to kick dust over his tracks.

The notes taken in the Wagner holdup are consigned to a bank in Helena, and as such, they are easily traced. Tips pour out of San Antonio like silt from a gold digger's pan. The bills turn up in every hotel and saloon along the sprawling dirt track of Main Street. Webb, who has anticipated the Wild Bunch escape from Montana, is already poking around Robber's Roost when a telegram finds him in Lander. Pinkerton is calling its agents to Texas.

Three days of hard riding over the arid plateaux land him on the doorstep of Fanny Price's Sporting House. Several agents are already in town, but they are following up a paper trail that Webb knows better to ignore. If the Pinkerton Head Office in Chicago has already received word, then Butch will be long gone. Cooling his heels in one of the isolated hideouts along the Outlaw Trail. Webb is in San Antonio for information only, and no barkeeper is going to give him what he is after.

However, Lillie Davis is only too accommodating when the lawman busts down her door at the Sporting House. She is in the middle of negotiations with a client when the hardware peels back the moulding and splinters the wood around the door's casing. She screams appropriately and then makes a half-hearted attempt to cover herself with the bedsheets. Her client thinks immediately to roll over and reach for his six-gun, but Webb places a well-aimed bullet into the still rocking headboard. Things calm afterward.

When the unfortunate cowhand has vacated the room, it is Lillie who speaks first. "He ain't here, as you can see fer yerself."

"No," Webb responds. "But you'll know where he is."

Webb is referring to Harvey Logan, and is only mildly surprised by what the woman has to say in response.

"I ain't heard nothin' from him in months."

The big man takes in the room with a quick sweep. Opens the woman's drawers and scatters her dainties over the floor. And then he finds it. An envelope. Webb cradles the boon in his hand.

"I'll save you the trouble," she continues. "It's cash all right— one hundred sixty-seven dollars to be exact. But it ain't from Wagner. I checked it out already."

Webb fingers the bills to corroborate the girl's story. In a town the size of San Antonio, Logan could easily have passed around enough money to make clean change in short order.

"How did you come by this much money, if it weren't Logan?"

"I ain't his property or somethin'. I got lots of admirers."

"Is that so? Why so precise an amount?"

"So's I can visit my ma back in Palestine."

Webb raises his eyebrows. The first threads of thought coming to him as he stands in the middle of the room.

"Maybe you ought to tell me just how you checked out this here money."

The girl's lips turn hard.

Sirango arrives in Fort Worth early the next day. The pressmen from Cheyenne are with him like lapdogs. He has his picture taken with the body of Deaf Charlie. Webb is not interviewed.

In 1901, Charles Sirango is already famous. Twenty years earlier, he helped Pat Garrett bring down Billy the Kid. He has already penned his first book, *A Texas Cowboy*, detailing his adventures with horse thieves and rustlers. He is a firm believer in his own mythology. A peddler of the Sirango mystique. A phrenologist told him at a young age that he was meant for detective work. And so he set out to become one.

He is an obsessive-compulsive. Tracking the brakeman from a Wells-Fargo heist clear into Mexico. Holing up in a hotel for weeks. Surviving on tequila and worms. Lying in wait, and eventually pouncing in Leavenworth, Texas. He was once hired by two wealthy mill owners to hunt down a man known only as "Tim." He turned Texas upside down and scoured the state of Oklahoma. Shaking down men of that name. Terrorizing unfortunate children, before he found the right one in Colorado.

However, he was best known by the newspapermen who followed him as a master of disguise. Posing as outlaws. Infiltrating their worlds and making love to their women. Feeling at home in their hats with the cold steel of a six-shooter hugging his hip. He once impersonated a miner to break up a circle of ore thieves. But in his business, you are only as good as your last arrest. And Sundance and Butch had eluded him. Wreaked havoc on his fragile mind.

After his conversation with Lillie, Webb rides through the night in the direction of Starr Valley. It seems that, indeed, there is no honour among thieves. Hanks had paid Logan's girl a visit in the other man's absence. It was not the story he expected to pick up, but the girl was telling the truth. He was sure. According to Lillie, the Bunch split up in order to confuse the posses, and no one has heard from Logan since. Hanks was gone now too, of course. He lit out for Wyoming after word about the marked bills began circulating, which meant that he was already a week ahead of the man from Pinkerton. But thanks to Lillie's new information, Webb has a pretty good idea about where to look.

Starr Valley is an obscure hideout that straddles the borders between Idaho and Wyoming. At first thought it seems an unlikely stopover, given its distance from San Antonio. But the puzzle is already beginning to reshape itself in Webb's mind. Logan's absence in Texas means that the Bunch split in the early running. They'd last been spotted cresting the Bearpaws, which would put Cassidy in easy striking distance of the Flaming Gorge pass and a free ticket into Utah.

Butch would know Starr Valley as a hideout for his family's polygamist brethren. And, of late, it has also become a haven for cattle rustlers as well. Tucked away in the mountains with easy access to the Salt River, it suddenly seems the obvious choice. And if Hanks lit out quickly, he might be hoping to catch Butch and Sundance there as a rendezvous point now.

Webb begins his search in Afton at a trading post owned by a man named Burton. It has taken several days to get here, with little rest, and Webb is in a foul mood. Burton crosses his arms over his burly chest and shrugs his shoulders in response to the lawman's initial inquiries. Webb smiles in spite of his fatigue. These are the moments that he cherishes about his line of work.

With his right foot, Webb sweeps the man's legs out from under him in one smooth motion. Burton hits the floorboards with a heavy crash, toppling a rack of canned goods, which cascade in turn, and roll about the man's corpulent mass. At the sound of Webb's pistol hammer slipping into place, Burton's eyes widen with horror. It doesn't take much more than that.

Three of the bandits had, as Webb deduced, ridden through here three weeks earlier. They'd stayed only a few days in a cabin about a mile to the north. Only Hanks had returned since.

"He was ascared. You could see that much. Not swaggering this time. Not without them other two at his side."

"Where is he now?" Webb says flatly.

"Shot his mouth off about going to Nashville."

"Nashville?"

"Yeah. Kept saying he'd be sipping drinks and shootin' pool in style while the law tore up the trail lookin' for him."

"When'd he leave?"

The 3rd Cavalry is disbanded in 1883, and Webb is a caged bear in the parlours of Chicago. For the first time in years, his hair is cropped and his beard is trimmed. The Indian Wars are over. The Sioux are sedated. But Laramie is still in his mind. He is a man with a uniform. A reputation. But no money. His men are gone. Discharged or transferred. The West has been won. And Webb has become an anachronism. His arms, like oak boughs, end in hands that curl awkwardly around teacups. Hands that have bled life from the warm bodies of Sioux. He finds his tongue clicking politely around words that seem foreign. Like, "Please." And, "Thank you." He is uneasy with women. He sweats and he blushes in their presence. Even the men here are strange. Like gelded stallions. Clipped and polished men in their Teddy boy suits. But there is nothing wild about their tails. They cover their nails with white gloves. And they smell. Like lavender and fresh laundry.

After an hour among them, he wants to break things. To shatter the cup in his hands. To lunge across the table with silverware and unseam the simpering fool on the other side.

But this is all before Rose. The white light. The debutante. Heir to the Deschamps industrial empire. She is the life raft in the wreck of his military career. For her, he will endure men that pat him on the back and say, "Webb, old boy. Kill any Indians lately?" He will listen as they turn him into a joke for their wives, and the young women after their fortunes.

For Rose, he moves to Chicago and succumbs to a dinner jacket. He sits quietly in the plush salons of rich matriarchs. Tries his tongue at small talk. He takes tea with her mother, and loses badly to her father at billiards. But most of all, he follows her like a tamed animal. He watches her.

In the world he comes from, men pay for their women and leave before morning. But Rose will never know such a world exists. She will travel to the civilized meccas of New York and London. Paris and Rome. And she will see nothing from her bubble of wealth. She speaks to Webb in the voice of a child. And in many ways, she will never grow old. When she allows him to sit beside her in public, he holds his breath. Afraid she might break into pieces. Her delicate bones click audibly beneath a thin veneer of translucent skin. It is as though he has been drugged and dragged into a private petting zoo. He is her favourite pet. Bound by the invisible chain of unrequited love.

But Webb is never entirely tamed. The drugs not strong enough. His senses whisper warnings to him everywhere he goes. But he buries them willingly. Suppresses them for her. And so he misses the cues. The signals like beacons.

And instead, he believes that he is seducing her. Entering her world like a door jamb. They ride the subway to rooms he cannot afford. They grunt and sweat with the shades drawn tight. But she is not so innocent. Not so coy as sly. The door is never really opened to him.

When Rose's engagement is announced, Webb can hear the voices of the powerful whispering at his neck. Their ironic speech like death. He is cowed. Brought low before them. Rooms go quiet when he enters. When he tries to gain access to Rose—to ask her why, to explain—she is off at a spa, or gone to the Hamptons for a retreat. Some even claim she is in Venice with an aunt.

His humiliation is complete. Broke and broken, he signs on with the Pinkerton Detective Agency. Returns south and west to the open lands. There are still people who will pay him to kill.

Webb is only in Nashville two days when a boy fetches him from his spot in a local saloon. He had spent the previous day kicking dust up and down the busy streets, flashing a mug shot of Hanks in every retail establishment, as well as passing out a list of numbered bills. His footwork had apparently paid off. The young lad was the son of a haberdasher. His father had received one of the bills in exchange for a new hat, and then he'd recognized the man's face. The boy said that his father hollered after Hanks and the man had set out at a run. Several citizens gave chase, but lost him in the canebrakes along the Cumberland River.

Webb gives the boy a coin and makes for the train station. He knows that Hanks will not leave town on foot, and that he will more than likely make his own way to the train. All Webb has to do is lie in wait. If he knows anything about Hanks, it is that he will do what is expected of him. So Webb drums his fingers waiting for the man and follows him clear back to Texas.

Later, word is sent. Webb is to join Sirango for a drink in his rooms at Fort Worth's finest hotel. When the big man arrives on time, Sirango greets him dressed in a smoking jacket.

"Please, have a seat, Webb."

Webb does not like him already. He is one of the powerful men. Like the geldings of Chicago, the power has spoiled whatever instinct was there before. He has the look of an expert lawman. The sort of man you could trust to capture Butch Cassidy. But Webb knows better. He can smell the laundered clothes.

"You've done the Pinkerton Detective Agency a great service, Webb," he says, extending the finely manicured hand. In it rests a box of Cuban cigars. Webb declines.

"Ah, you don't know what you're missing, Webb."

He cannot stand the way the man uses his name like a secret handshake.

"We've got some reports about a murder in Montana." Sirango takes a long drag off his own cigar. "A rancher by the name of Jim Winters."

Webb shifts in his chair. He feels uneasy in the enclosed space of the room. Far too much hand-carved mahogany. Cut-glass light fixtures. A mirror behind the desk attempts to add depth, but only reflects the same stultifying decor. The cigar smoke sliding around Sirango like an oil slick bothers Webb's eyes.

"I want you to investigate, Webb. I'll clean up things down here."

Webb understands the man's motives clearly. This is a wild goose chase. A bone for the dog. Cassidy could not possibly be in Montana.

"With all due respect, Mr. Sirango, my instincts tell me Cassidy is in Texas. Or at least, he was so recently."

Sirango is not fazed. He leans back in his chair by the window and removes the cigar from his mouth. In its place, he sticks a smile.

"I'm sure you're right, Webb. Instincts like yours are meant to be trusted. But I've got a train full of agents at my disposal down here. He won't escape me. I can promise you that."

Webb's face contracts as he bites down hard to master his temper. There is a letter opener on the desk. In two moves, the man in front of him could be dead. Sirango has backed him into a corner. If he protests, it will seem as though he wants the credit for himself. If he leaves without a word, Sirango will get credit for the work he has done. Or worse. Cassidy will slip through the soft man's fingers.

After another pull on the Cuban cigar, Sirango continues. Pressing his advantage.

"My sources tell me Kid Curry is behind the killing. If that's the case, you may find other members of the Wild Bunch with him. It could mean a promotion for you." Behind the man's smile his tongue flickers. Not unlike a snake.

When Webb leaves the office, he does not return to his own room, but to the livery. The old buckskin stallion he rode in on is waiting.

Writing-on-Stone

THE BOY IN THE NEXT ROOM IS SLEEPING. SHE HAS WATCHED HIM
for days. The innocent rise of his bandaged chest. The delicate
mouth. Red lips, full as a rose. His eyes flutter as he dreams. She
could watch Robert for hours too. But the sleep was different.
Brought on by staggering fatigue. A deep slumbering waste without dreams. The sleep of exhaustion, after hours spent in the sun.
Recording, searching. Reaching backward in time. Fifty sites
along the coulee wall. One hundred thousand figures. One, two,
three thousand years of civilization scratched into stone. Wars
and coronations. Hunting parties and wedding ceremonies. And
of course, the medicine wheels. A scientist's playground. And no
one willing to call him in to dinner. At least no one he would listen to.

Veccha takes water from the stove and fills the metal tub in the
middle of the room. A liquid island. The steam builds moisture
on the rafters. She has not slept since the boy's arrival. Since she
shot him full of salt and rusty nails. She pulls the cotton dress up
and over her head. The warm glow of the lamp and the mere

knowledge of the boy are enough to heighten the intimacy of bathing. Render the common erotic. And suddenly, she is aware of herself in a way that is new. The broad hips of flesh. The delicate feet. She is instantly flushed. Aware of her own beauty. A word she would not have used in the past to describe the big-boned expanse of her frame. And yet this evening, it is all she can do to ignore it.

Robert had enjoyed her. Had found her attractive. But he had not understood what it was to love a woman. He addressed only the physical need. As though it were something to be endured. Something that interfered with his mind. Slowed him at work. He crawled beneath the sheets hard and intent. The same way he approached the coulee wall. Not out of curiosity. Out of desire. He did not luxuriate in the process of discovery. In the beauty that only art and nature provided. Rather he operated on the urge to discover itself. The need to collect and record. To explain and conquer and reify. The need to control.

Veccha feels differently about the petroglyphs. The pictographs and the medicine wheels. For her, they are an affirmation. A product of passion. The sheer aura of desire. The power of their creation feeds her. The first time Robert took her to the site, she laid her hand upon the etching of a bison. Its cool warmth more like a dream than an indifferent stone. A celebration of life.

And the power she felt on the wall is apparent to her in every corner of the Milk River valley. Two Bears shares this knowledge with her. Although he would not describe it in so many words. *This is where I am buried*, he would say. *This is my home.*

The warm water enters her pores like a drug. Soothing the tired muscles, tighter than fists. Her body draws in the warmth of the steam until the air becomes cool to the touch. Her skin contracts. And the pores close. Her belly is tight as a drum. And the room breathes like a tent. A moth-like pulsing of wings.

The wind coming in over the open sill of the window is what finally awakens him. He is lying on his back in the straw-filled bed beneath him. His chest is bare, and the sheets have been turned down to alleviate heat. His shoulder has been wrapped in makeshift bandages. It is sore to the touch. He makes no effort to move. He can smell the distinct scent of lye on his skin. Vaguely, he remembers being shot.

It is early evening outside. Only a faint afterglow of sunshine bleeds into the room. The lazy slap of the windmill's turning. The scent of baked dust. On the far side of a partially drawn curtain, a lamp burns. Throwing its arms across the wall and partway across the ceiling.

After the initial moments of confusion pass, Wyoming is aware of sound. Someone in the next room pours water. With a little effort, he is able to lean past the extent of the curtain without harming his shoulder. A woman is standing in the middle of the floor. Her feet are hidden from view. Concealed by the metallic walls of a tub. She is otherwise naked. Posed like women in the erotic photographs shown to him by Flat-Nosed Curry.

Her arms are extended over her head. Lifting the visible breast toward the light of the lamp. She is bent slightly to the left, and her body slopes gently into the raised hip of her ass and back toward the length of her leg. She is facing away in three-quarter profile. Wringing water from the mass of her long hair. The droplets roll back down the concave track of her spine.

This is what he sees in the dreamlike state of wakefulness. In the moments before he slips backward into the darkness of a necessary sleep. Cold running water on the prairie.

Two Bears saw the boy wandering lost in a land of hoodoos. He was a half-day's ride to the south along the Milk River. Coup Stick suggested that they kill him and leave his body for the birds, but Two Bears ignored this. His younger brother has a penchant for rash action, and his hatred of the white man is well known. Two Bears, and his youngest sibling, Red Cloud, are much more methodical in their hatred. And besides, this boy, he knows, is the work of Napiw, the Old Man. His coming signals the end of things. But in the way of all endings, this boy will also be a new beginning. This is the way Napiw intended the world to be.

Two Bears knows that eventually he will have to move north and west. Follow the trail of his people. There is no life for him here. The buffalo are long gone. But this valley is a sacred place, and it is a sadness to him to leave it. Nevertheless, he might have left it earlier had it not been for the witch-woman. The white shaman and her magic.

Two Bears feels a certain duty toward her that he cannot explain. A need to watch over her. For though her skin may be white, she is one of them in a much deeper way. His brothers cannot agree, but they stay because of his vision. A vision of the last gathering. The Ghost Dance led by a witch-woman.

Two Bears expects Veccha to know this vision also, because she can see so many things. But she could offer him nothing for its telling. So he stays and he waits with his brothers.

It cannot be long now, he thinks. This boy is the omen he has been looking for. It does not matter that the white shaman is blind to him. Napiw works in strange ways.

She carries the lantern in front of her face. A bubble of light in the night. From a distance, someone might mistake her for a firefly, alone in the dark of the prairie. Burning. She allows herself this indulgence—this walking at night—because she cannot have the bed. Or so she tells herself. But she has done it before while Robert was sleeping. Nonetheless, it makes her feel good to believe in the lie.

She does not consider the possible dangers as she follows the well-worn path to the wall. The warm eyes of the wolves stationed upon her. She thinks only of what awaits her like a chapter in her favourite book. Eager to turn the page. She wonders, for a moment, if Two Bears has ever caught her in this act. If he watches over the wolves. And if he has—if he does—why then does he not join her in this pilgrimage?

But then her thoughts turn to the boy in her bed. His bandaged chest. The wound that she gave him. She is concerned—not about his origins or that he might be dangerous—but that she did not anticipate his arrival. Did not dream him, as Two Bears suggested.

When she reaches the wall, it is transformed into a garden of shadows by the light of her lamp. The rock carvings become liquid. Are sent into motion. Herds of buffalo rumble over stone as though she has turned back the clock on their disappearance. Hunters on horseback give chase. Two Bears told her that the Peigan elders often came here for guidance. Searching the artworks for portents. Adding new works of their own. Perhaps this is why she feels so safe here. So at home in the neighbourless expanse of the prairie. Like those elders, she finds a certain kinship with the wall. As though it were a lightning rod for her own clairvoyance.

And just as she thinks this, there is a new carving. A figure she has overlooked. It would not have been difficult to miss it in the past. Despite her meticulous inspection. Her careful reading. It is filed away by the wind and partially obscured by an outcropping of stone, so that the light of the lamp—the shadow it casts—is what brings it to her attention. It is a man. A V-neck body. And he is alone on the burnt stone of the prairie.

Even in sleep, the boy is so stubborn, she cannot remove his boots. And so she must bathe him by hand. Drawing water from a clay jug. Lightly she brushes dust away from his chest. A film so fine it finds its way through the closed window. Accumulating over time. As invasive as germs. When his eyes flutter, she assumes he is dreaming again. As he so often does. Speaking and crying, sometimes. So much like a child. And barely more than that. But he is not dreaming. He is surfacing. Entering the waking world.

"You shot me." The first thing he says.

"Yes."

"I ain't never been shot before." And he looks into her face. The broad high cheeks. The white down on her lip. "You've got two eyes."

Her brow wrinkles in response.

"I mean two different colours. One's blue. And the other ... it's brown. With green. And yellow."

"Does your shoulder still hurt?"

"Eh? Nah. It feels purty good. You're a heckuva shot."

"No. I was aiming to kill you."

There is something odd about her voice he cannot quite place. Not so much an accent as an inflection. As though everything were a question. He knew an old Swedish stablebuck who spoke that way.

"Good thing you missed."

His smile is an evil thing, diffused by his eyes. Even lying perfectly still there is an energy, a restlessness, humming through his bones. She expects him to leap from the bed to the floor and dance out a jig to show her that he is fine.

"There is soup," she tells him, but again it sounds like a question.

"By my nose, I do believe that there is." He beams at her from his roost on the pillow.

Robert noticed her eyes the second time they made love.

Two Bears looks down into the Milk River coulee. Thin plumes of smoke rise from the shaman's cabin. Last night he sought guidance from Napiw. And he knows that he must remain here a while longer. But the days are numbered now.

Many of the Peigan have lost faith in the Old Man since he has gone into the mountains and ceases to show himself, but Two Bears persists in his belief. The disenchanted say Napiw would never have allowed the sickness and the hunger to befall his people, but Two Bears believes in cycles. His faith will not fail him for this reason.

The elders still speak of the Old Man often, even though the young buffalo braves have turned away. They say Napiw entered this land from the south, creating the mountains and the plains the way he saw them. It was Napiw who planted the forests and the grasses. And it was he who dredged the Milk River. Stones are buried in the earth just to the north, where it is said that the Old Man lay down to rest his tired bones after crossing its keen waters. These stones are strewn in his image and are visible even now.

It was Napiw who made the animals and provided for them the fruits of the earth, like camas and carrots, berries and roots. He put the bighorn sheep in the mountains and the buffalo on the prairies.

When he was through with these things, he took clay from the earth and moulded the figures of woman and child. These he covered with a stone and went away. But when the Old Man returned from his journey, he uncovered his creations and gave them a name.

"Arise," he said. "You shall be people."

Napiw lived among the Peigan for a long time, for they had much to learn and he had much to teach them. But eventually, the Old Man grew tired and slouched off into the West. The faithful, like Two Bears, say that he shall return some day, and when he does, he will bring the buffalo with him.

For it is said that he knows where the white man has hidden them.

Two Bears urges his horse away from the cliff and sets off to awaken his brothers.

For two more days, Wyoming sleeps on his back, trapped in the close air of the room. Veccha feeds him meals and sponges the ever-present dust from his torso. On the morning of the third day, she arrives with bread and salt pork. Leftovers from the meal the night before. He is asleep. Has not awakened at all today. His eyelids flutter under the weight of a dream.

Veccha sits on the corner of the bed. Sets the food on the floor. Wyoming's body is stiff as a board. She reaches out with the index finger of her right hand, testing the puckered skin of the forming scars. Their lumpy sureness like an affirmation. His body is sinew and bone. Spare. She did not expect to find another man in her bed so soon. Or ever. The hand lingers in the fine blond hairs between his nipples. It is then that she sees he is awake. Staring at the hand on his chest. She pulls back as though burned.

"You are well now. You should get up." Her tone is perfunctory. Cross. As though she has been tricked or caught in the act of something shameful.

Wyoming closes his eyes and settles deeper into the mattress. "Is that plate for me?"

"No." Her face flushes with the lie. "Yours is set on the table. When you are ready to rise."

She leaves him there. Brushing through the drawn curtain like wind through a wash.

At the dinner table he is live animation. He speaks with his mouth full. His arms shoot off in every direction. Jerking and stumbling like a bull calf. Watching Wyoming is like being party to a perpetual puppet show, she thinks. She hails from a family of silence. Of thinkers. Of serious farmers. She has never witnessed such unchained elation. And at first she is frightened. Afraid he will burst. Or that his limbs will come unhinged. Land on the floor. Robert could not have used so many words in a lifetime.

"They thought to keep me otherwise occupied by hiding my clothes. But I didn't care none. I didn't intend to give up my share of the loot. Heck, if they'd of been serious about keepin' me outa the way, they'd of had better luck with a three-pound sledge. And even then . . . no ma'am, I'd of crawled buck naked in chains for a piece of that action."

He is a thief, she understands now. It is a fact he does not hide. A fact that he celebrates. She has heard of this Butch and Sundance. Read stories in the paper. Followed their worlds with haphazard fascination. It is the way that she absorbs life. Through itinerant stories. Bits and pieces. But Wyoming offers her the whole rush of history. Spits it up like unchewed food on the table.

"We'd struck camp on the banks of the Humboldt River," he explains while administering another forkful. "It was Bill Carver's idea to hide my clothes. He poked fun at me the night before for takin' 'em off. But it was Indian summer that year. Too damn hot to sleep in your trousers and shirt.

"Oh, pardon my language.

"By the time I got to Winnemucca, they were already piling out the back door with the cash in potato sack bags and a box of gold bricks.

"Carver took one look at me, and damn near . . . I mean, he dang near fell off his horse with hilarity. Dropped the gold right there in the street. Well, he got down off that useless plug mare and she turned all skittish with the commotion. He done had two hands on the gold. One foot in the stirrups. And she just kept shyin' away like the coy girl at a dance. Ol' Bill just skippin' along beside her like a one-legged man."

The boy's humour is contagious. Veccha smiles before she has a chance to swallow it down.

"What did he do then?"

"Well, if things wasn't bad enough for him, the bank manager come out all puffed up with hisself totin' a revolver. And some dirt farmer come with him carryin' a shotgun. They put out two windows in the saloon across the street, before the barkeeper screamed at 'em to stop before they kilt someone.

"'Course Carver's horse is long gone by then. So in comes me to the rescue in my skivvies and boots. A more unlikely hero you never saw. I give some old lady the wink as we rode past her and into the dust cloud Butch left us."

"Were you chased?"

"Clear into Utah," he tells her before diving back into cold chicken stew.

Not long after the Winnemucca holdup, the Bunch made its way to Fort Worth, Texas. The intention being to lay low in a place called Hell's Half Acre. But the four outlaws ran into Harvey Logan and Ben Kilpatrick. Flush with their take and tired of life on the lam, each of them bought new outfits, including derby hats and gold watch fobs. Butch even went so far as to purchase a bicycle, as they were all the rage.

So pleased with themselves, they decided to stop at a photographer's shop to have their likenesses taken. Wyoming did not think that it was one of Butch's better ideas. The lawmen were still hot over their last job in Nevada. But Butch was in such high spirits that he ignored the boy's warning.

"If you don't want to be seen with us, then the least you can do is watch over my bicycle while we're inside."

Butch would later ditch the bicycle in a fury following a riding accident, but that photograph would be displayed in the shop's window for days afterward. And it wasn't long before a sharp-eyed detective from Wells Fargo recognized Bill Carver from a previous likeness. Back at the main office, the four other men were quickly identified, and an entire detachment of lawmen was loosed in the area.

The celebrations were cut short under the circumstances, and the core members of the Wild Bunch, including Wyoming, blew town once again for their hideout in Robber's Roost.

Two Bears is an odd name for a Peigan. But that is the name Napiw chose for him. Two Bears travelled north to Big Rock in the summer of his twelfth year to take his vision quest. The quartzite boulder is visible for miles, and has always been a sacred site to his people. It has been told that Napiw himself came to rest at this spot, but finding the stone too hot, threw down his coat as a blanket.

Napiw was so pleased with the rock's hospitality that he elected to leave him the coat, because he was poor. Only as Napiw trekked northward, it began to rain and he was forced to return for the garment. The rock, however, refused to give up the coat. Napiw was enraged and stole it back anyway. To his surprise, the boulder lifted itself from the earth and chased him down. The animals Napiw had created came to his aid, but were crushed in the rock's path. Finally, it was a bat that flew into the stone and cracked it. The boulder came to a rest in two pieces. It never moved again.

Two Bears could see the crevasse separating the rock when he arrived alone and hungry. He built a U-shaped shelter atop the hill from surrounding stones. He sat there, hidden from the wind, to await his vision. But several days passed with nothing. On the morning of the third day, Two Bears thought he heard an eagle cry, but when he stood up to inspect the noise, his legs would not support him. All day he lay beneath the sun without food or water. He had come all this way to find an auspicious vision, and still he had nothing. He felt that even if he were to manage the strength, he could not return to his village without having experienced a vision. It would be shameful.

That night was the longest night of his life. The stars were covered and no light came to him. The temperature had fallen off from the daytime heat. He was shivering. Just when he thought that he might die if he did not leave in search of food, his vision came with the sun. Two prairie grizzlies stood on the plain beneath him. Facing off. He lay quite still so as not to attract their attention. It was a rare sight to see the grizzly like this. To have two was certainly a sign of good luck.

The bears fought a terrible battle for the better part of the day. And eventually after many hours the larger bear gave up and lumbered west toward the mountains. The remaining bear trembled before the young boy's eyes and became a woman. A shaman. And she called to Two Bears and all his people. She would lead them in one last Sundance. It would be a Ghost Dance, she told him. For the end of things. And for the things to come.

Two Bears was rejuvenated by the vision, and he returned to his village the next day with its telling. There, he was given his name. And the elders told him that it was a gift from the Old Man.

Constable Whitfield of the Northwest Mounted Police arrives unannounced one morning after Wyoming is walking again. He is wearing the telltale red serge tunic and Montana peak of his office. Veccha is bent over in the garden when she first hears his greeting, and her heart skips a beat. Her hand, which wrestles with a well-established weed, halts in suspended animation. Wyoming is in the barn, or at least he was moving that way the last time she saw him. A single drop of cool perspiration runs the length of her torso. She can feel the blood in her neck. Veccha realizes that she has hesitated too long in responding and continues to pry at the weed, feigning ignorance. When the constable shouts a second time, Veccha forces herself to stand and smile a greeting in return.

She is somewhat unclear about the nature of her fear. The constable is well known to her, and as she is the only homestead in this area, he makes a habit of including her home on his patrol. But Wyoming is admittedly a criminal. Can the visit be nothing more than a benign coincidence? She wonders if he has heard the constable arriving, or whether he will step into the yard at any second. What will she say if he does?

"You are out early this morning, yes," Veccha says as the constable's horse draws alongside the edge of her garden. The small rabbit-proof fence between them.

"Couldn't sleep." His boots are buffed to a high polish. The uniform immaculate. But the hat is pulled low to shadow his face, and his jovial manner is at odds with what she sees beneath.

"You are sick?" Veccha inquires, understanding the true state of affairs.

"Self-inflicted, I'm afraid."

The history of the Northwest Mounted Police in Milk River dates back to the first march west. The troops camped four days along its quiet shores as they awaited supplies from forts in the Dakota Territory. The men discovered the ancient rock carvings along the coulee walls during their stopover. Veccha has witnessed their transgressions. Names scrawled haphazardly into the sandstone cliffs. Lewd remarks improperly spelled.

In the summer of 1887, the Mounties returned with their tents and established a temporary post in anticipation of supposed smuggling activity and trouble from the mining camps in Butte. That post eventually became a permanent fixture in 1889 with the building of a log cabin. Meant as part of a complex border patrol system, it never did house more than twelve constables at any one time, and was soon reduced to its current three-man

headquarters. Desertion remains a problem. Alcoholism brought
on by loneliness.

But Veccha trusts Constable Whitfield's intentions even if he
does ride a little crooked in the saddle from time to time.

"Anyway, I'm headed north today," the constable adds. "In
need of some supplies at the cabin. Thought you might wish to
send a message to your brothers."

Veccha realizes that she has been holding her breath only as
she lets it go. The muscles in her neck soften. "Tell them that
there is a section of fence to be mended. My regards to Father."

"Thinking to stay on then, are you?" Constable Whitfield's
tone suggests a note of incredulity.

"I have you to protect me, yes?"

The man blushes. "I ought to go now."

"You won't stay for tea?" It is a risk she takes with the question,
but she cannot do otherwise. On the prairie your neighbours are
seldom about. The extension of hospitality would be expected.

"No, thank you. It's a long ride."

As the constable moves on, Veccha returns to her work. Dip-
ping her hands in the warm loam of the soil. She does not hazard
a look to the barn, and yet somehow she knows that if she does,
the boy will be watching her.

The world of her cabin is essentially spare. Like the rooms of a
monk or another aesthete. The only point of ostentation is the
shelf of books. A small collection of coloured bindings piled
neatly in rows. It is not the first thing he notices. In fact,
Wyoming has been here for days and only discovered them now.
Were he able to read the gilded lettering on their spines, he
would find *The Origin of the Species* by Charles Darwin and *Mysteries of the Antique World* by Lord Gavin Risk. They would mean
nothing to him, even if he could read.

Out of curiosity and boredom, he reaches for a copy of *The Flora of Australia.* He is delighted, at first, to discover a selection of black and white plates. But is immediately disappointed upon further investigation to discover the drawings are exclusively of flowers. Most of which he does not recognize. He wonders then, before replacing the volume in its space on the shelf, what other secrets are locked in the pages of these books. In the volumes that have no pictures at all. It is not the first time that he has considered this. But in the past the thought had been fleeting. He wondered only obliquely. Today, it seems particularly important that he know.

Perhaps it is only due to his current need of a scribe. The ability to write. But he is not so sure. It seems to him that if someone has taken the time to create so many words, they must have something important to say.

He had the Bible read to him as a child in church. And although he cannot remember much about what he was told, he knows that there were lessons. Morals, they call them. And he remembers that there were patterns that ran through those stories. Things that happened time and time again. It seems to Wyoming, as he stands before her altar of books—their special place in the cabin—that the right book might have a story like his story. That maybe this has happened before. And suddenly, he would like very much to have that book. To be able to read the next page.

Veccha makes him sit quietly in the bedroom on Sunday, while she ministers to the small flock of seekers on her doorstep. All morning he sits cross-legged on the bed listening to her speak. Sometimes in English. More often in the Norwegian tongue of her childhood. He imagines the faces of her seekers. Their sad, hopeful gazes. Even when he cannot understand what they ask, he finds the sorrow in their voices draining. But he is entranced by the process. Drawn to it like he is drawn to danger.

Finally, he can sit still no longer. And rising quietly like a stalking cat, he approaches the curtain. The voice drifting softly through the cotton drape is oddly familiar. But he cannot imagine its speaker, though he tries. In the end, his curiosity wins out, and he pushes through. Just enough to take in the room.

Veccha's back is toward him. Her head is lowered in thought. And across the stark white of the table's apron sits a young woman. Her hands twist furiously in the ribbons of her dress. She is dark-haired and slender. Her skin is pale, and she wears too much makeup. She appears to Wyoming as a child playing dress-up. He has only a moment to decide that she is pretty before she lifts her eyes to his face. Two dark pools, and instantly he understands who she is. Where she is from.

He closes the curtain then and returns to the bed. Sitting on the edge with his feet on the floor, Wyoming lays his head in his hands.

When the last of the visitors leaves, Veccha comes to him without an explanation. She does not mention the seekers at all.

"You must be hungry," she says in the schoolteacher voice she first used with him days ago. "Come. I will feed you."

She is not aware that he has been seen.

In the kitchen, she is economy in motion. No movements are extraneous. Nothing she does is without purpose. She extracts the potatoes from a bin under the table and prepares them for paring.

Wyoming does not know where to begin.

"What do you see in my future?" he asks her. And his question is swallowed in the silence between. The hesitation. A call drifts in through the window, and the last team of horses pulls out. The rickety bump and crack of the wagon slowly recedes. Veccha blinks.

"What do you say?"

"Who were those people? How do you know what to tell them?"

Veccha cries out in response, as the long thin blade of the knife opens her thumb. Dark warm blood leaks in slow rivers. She turns to him staring, the widening eyes of surprise. And before he can think, Wyoming places the damaged digit in the warmth of his mouth. They stand like this until the finger stops bleeding.

Two Bears watches the boy feed chickens in the yard. He has been watching for several days now. At first, the Indian was careful not to be seen, but he has come to realize that the boy cannot see, and so he watches unabashedly in the daylight now. He is not like the other white men. This much is clear. But his arrival—Napiw's bringing of this trickster—is a mystery to him still.

Two Bears was only a boy when he saw his first white man. A tall wiry man with a pot-belly and hair on his face. Much like the buffalo. But he was oily and smelt like the burnt flesh of a pig. The boy did not like him. But his father seemed to know the man, and greeted him oddly with a shaking of hands and much back slapping.

"He comes from the fort," his mother told him.

Word of the new fort had reached his village early in the spring. It was built at the confluence of the Oldman and St. Mary's rivers. It was a place only his father and a handful of others had visited. Each time the men returned from their trips to the fort, they brought with them trade goods and treasure. Trinkets bought with the season's fur harvest. The elders were not happy with the trades and swore off the evil objects. They cursed Two Bears's father for over-hunting.

"There will be no more buffalo," they warned. "And we will be slaves to the white man's charms."

Some of these older men still fashioned their arrowheads with

the ancient hammerstones of their ancestors. But Two Bears's
father dismissed them with a wave of his hand. He was a proud
man. And his journeys to the fort became more frequent. Each
time the trading party left, more men would go with them. And
the more men who went, the longer they stayed away.

At first, his father brought back blankets and tools. He provided his wife with a looking glass. And to his eldest son, he gave
a knife. Two Bears marvelled at the strength and accuracy of its
edge. He thought that the elders were crazy. But after a time, his
father came back with the firewater. And there would be such a
noise at their gatherings. His father would dance with the other
men from the party and pass the bottle between them like friends.
Until it was gone, and the fighting began. The pointing of fingers. The elders remained in their tents during these times. They
passed the pipe and made their own plans.

One night his father stumbled drunk into the campfire, scattering sparks into the air like flaming birds. For days, Two Bears's
mother nursed the boiling flesh on the wounded man's backside.
The elders gave him shameful names to live with, and Two Bears
bore the taunting of the older village boys. He begged his father
not to go back to the fort, but it was not to be. In the fall, the
trading party was bigger than ever. There were even plans to
move the village closer for the winter.

And then his father gave up the hunt. He spent much of his
time with the white man, instead. Tracking bear and other big
game for their sport. Living off their meagre offerings and booze.
He became the pig man's errand boy. And Two Bears's family
members were forced to accept the charity of their neighbours.

From time to time squabbles broke out amongst the plains
Indians and the operatives of the whiskey fort they called Hamilton. A blanket would go missing. A bowl. Or perhaps a bottle of
their precious firewater. And there would be repercussions. Beat-
ings. Many turned from the white man then. But not his father.
He had already begun to wear boots and a top hat. Cast-offs from

the fort. Often it was reported that he was seen stumbling blind drunk outside its walls, screaming for the white man's whiskey. Two Bears was almost a man then, and his people had stood quietly by for too long.

Painted and wearing their war bonnets, they converged upon the fort before winter. A battle ensued and Two Bears killed a man in the confusion. A young white boy, not much older than himself, with long red hair and a pale face ruined with pimples. Two Bears put the steel gift-knife of his father's giving between the ribs of the young man's chest, and he watched the light slowly disappear from his eyes.

In the end, the Peigan razed the fort to the ground in a bonfire visible for many miles around. They swept it from the prairie in a billow of black smoke. Even now Two Bears remembers the dancing, the singing that ensued past dark. He took his first woman that night in the heat of his family's tipi. It had been a good day.

But the next morning, he was awakened by the hand of a friend. And brought away from the warmth of his woman to the ruins of the fort. Still smoking in the pink globe of the rising sun. And there he looked upon the wasted flesh of his own father. Crying like a child as he searched through the charred timbers for a bottle of the white man's whiskey. His own hands burnt beyond all recognition.

Early the next year, they built a new fort. And the white man called it Whoop Up.

Perhaps Coup Stick was right, he thinks. Maybe they should have killed this boy too.

The first time Wyoming dropped out of the sky, he landed on the back of the Overland Flyer, nine miles west of Rock Creek. Between Leroy and Wilcox. Logan had him do it at night. It was his idea of an initiation. What Logan had not bet on was the boy's natural talent for falling.

The summer before he had been chasing down mustangs. Riding in shifts with three other men. The following day, they would lead them captive to the coral, where the process would begin. Mounting the horse was a difficult task. Staying atop was next to impossible. In the early days Wyoming would return to the bunkhouse beaten and bruised. He smashed up his wrist. Dislocated his jaw. But he did not give up.

Some men know how to whisper to horses. Others wear them down through sheer determination. It got to the point Wyoming could calculate a forward pitch just right. Shift in the air. Succumb to inertia. And when it came to landing on his feet, he embarrassed the cat. Work on the ranch stopped in the afternoons. The coral became a carnival. The stablebuck set odds and collected the bets.

The train was only a natural progression. And although it may well have been faster than the average bronco, the train was decidedly more predictable. Unlikely to buck or pitch.

So at 2:18 a.m. on June 2, 1899, Logan watched on as Wyoming turned falling into art.

The horse is an integral part of the cowboy's identity. As inseparable from his image as the sugar-loaf sombrero, the six-gun, or the lariat. But like the other items of his personality, the horse is a tool. A necessity. Utilitarian in its nature. The wide brim of the cowboy's hat keeps the sun from his face. The rain off his shoulders. The six-gun is a portable weapon, unlike the rifle or the carbine, which are too cumbersome on roundup and are always a danger near the reins. He can use the six-gun to scare off wolves or to put down lame animals on the range. And the lariat allows a one-hundred-and-forty-pound man to rope and contain an animal ten times his weight.

But without the horse these other items are mere affectations.

It is the horse that creates the cowboy. Allows him to cover hundreds and thousands of miles on drives. It sets him up above the plain so that he can watch over the herd in his care. See Indian raiding parties and predators from miles away.

In spite of all this, the animal is treated with little affection. Most cowboys do not own their own horse. Are provided with one by their employer. And even when they do ride a horse of their own purchase, it rarely lasts more than seven years in his service. In fact, under emergency circumstances, the horse can be ridden to death in a single drive. Even under the best of conditions the animal is subject to all forms of abuse. Not the least of which is the spur or the whip.

The average cow pony is half wild. Descended from the Spanish breeds brought over with Columbus. A feral horse allowed to free range until the age of four years or so. Subsisting on wild grasses and scrub. Travelling in packs. Mustangs, they are called, from the Spanish word for "stray." An appropriate moniker, given their ornery nature.

Much effort is put into breaking these animals. A practice that involves several days of intensive discipline and training. A literal breaking of the will. Or at least a bending.

The average cowboy spends so much of his life riding that quite often he develops an aversion to walking, and begrudges even travelling the shortest of distances on foot. The horse provides him with a sense of power. Sets him above his fellow man. Cowboys even begin to look on horseless citizens with a note of disdain. As someone not truly of the West.

The cowboy, because of the nature of his employment, is a necessarily young and self-conscious braggart. As affected as an English dandy in his own way. And the horse is his most distinguished garment. In fact, when the value of the horse diminishes, when the railroad supplants the need for long-distance drives—shrinks the West to a fraction of its former self—the cowboy will disappear just as quickly as his trusty steed.

Veccha likes to watch him with the picture books. The same dog-eared copies of dime-store novels. Time after time. *The Adventures of Billy the Kid. Frontier Tales. Wide Awake Library.* He carries them everywhere, like a security blanket. Mornings down by the water under the shade of cottonwood boughs. In the cool mouth of the barn by late afternoon. Even nights by the light of her coal oil lamp. While she cleans dishes. Tidies the room.

She has picked them up herself when he was not looking. And for the first time, she can understand their magnetism. Not just academically, either. They are, she sees now, like a retelling of the old myths. The heroic epics of her own ancestors played out on the American frontier with the same flare for romanticism and hyperbole. The same yearning for melodrama.

These stories remind her of the boy, in fact. He exudes the same longing for adventure and abandon. She admires this quality in him. And yet, at the same time it scares her. When you grow used to control, to knowing—like it or not, you come to depend on it.

Wyoming does not have to read in order to understand fiction. He is intimate with the story of Billy the Kid. The magician who performed his famous escape from the Lincoln County jailhouse on the day of Wyoming's birth. He does not harbour any illusions about the Kid's character. He knows that Billy was not much more than a thug. A hired gun in a commercial war between the Murphy-Dolan faction and the enterprises of Tunstall and McSween. Merchant families fighting over a small piece of a very small pie. Billy was a killer. There is no doubt.

He was convicted of murdering Sheriff Brady in a trial that took only one day. But fate gave Billy small hands and too much opportunity. His jailhouse guards, for example, were even stupider than he. While the majority of the jail was across the street having dinner, Billy convinced poor old William Bell to take him to the privy. On his way back across the yard, Billy slipped the cuffs in the way he had in the past—simply by pulling them over his hands—and then used them as a flail to topple Bell. He then used the man's own pistol to finish him off.

Billy flew upstairs to Garrett's office then, and loaded the sheriff's own shotgun. On the balcony of the jailhouse, he waited for Ollinger, the other guard, to come running in response to his earlier shot. And when he did, Billy cut him down in mid-flight, in the middle of the street. The only thing is, Billy didn't stop there. He stole two more revolvers from Garrett's office and proceeded to dance a jig on the balcony, firing indiscriminately into the air. He stayed an hour before deciding to leave.

Sheriff Pat Garrett finally brought him down a few months later, literally with a shot in the dark. The boy's last words were, "Quien es?" Spanish for "who's there?"

It is the newspapers who created the boy's glorious outlaw image. In the same way they mythologize Butch and Sundance. But that is what attracts Wyoming to the stories. He is not interested in the facts of the outlaw's existence. He is in love with the romance. The making of a legend. The possibility of something greater.

Were it not for the marvellous transformational process of history, William Antrim—aka Henry McCarty, aka William H. Bonny, aka Billy the Kid—would remain a slow-witted, bucktoothed murderer. But instead, he is the stuff that dreams are made of. A much more interesting tale.

One year after Fort Hamilton was burnt, Two Bears heard a story from Blood traders in the south. What the great eastern newspapers were referring to as the Marias Massacre. Although he did not know it then, this event would mark the end of Blackfoot resistance to the white man. And his raid on the fort would be the last great Blackfoot victory in all of North America.

News from the Bloods was not so glorious.

On January 23rd, 1870, six companies of US cavalry—two hundred men all told—dismounted and crawled forward to the edge of a snowy bluff overlooking the Marias River. Below, still in the daze of early morning ablutions, was the winter camp of Peigan Chief Heavy Runner. He had blessed his warriors the night before and sent them out on a hunting expedition at dawn of that same morning. A little more than three hundred Indians remained in the camp. Most of them women and children and men too old or too sick to hunt. The small band was already in the grip of the white man's smallpox.

Major Eugene Baker was at the head of the military detachment that morning. And because he was cursed with the same affliction shared by Two Bears's father, he was drunk. He was on strict orders from General William Tecumseh Sherman to find and eliminate any and all Blackfoot resistance in the north. The band he was seeking specifically was that of Peigan leader Mountain Chief. In spite of the warnings given him from his scouts that this was not Mountain Chief's camp, Major Baker ordered his men to ready their .50 calibre guns.

Heavy Runner, alerted to their presence, lumbered forth onto the black silt flats of the Marias, now covered in a blanket of fresh white snow. In his hand, he held the papers of safe conduct given to him by the Indian Agent. Papers that granted him passage through his ancestors' land. Nervous, and too young for service, Private Joe Cobell fired the first shot. Heavy Runner slumped over like a felled bear. The papers still tight in his hand.

The .50 calibre guns opened then. Tearing through the tipi poles and shredding the buffalo hide of their tents. Many were smothered as the flames of their cook fires caught on the walls of their collapsed homes. The cavalry descended to the sounds of the Peigan women screaming. Desperate, the squaws lay upon their children to protect them from the rain of bullets. But the horsemen simply rode over them or finished them off with a shot from their Springfield rifles as they passed by.

Lieutenant William Pease counted two hundred Peigan bodies at raid's end. Private Walton MacKay, a Canadian, was the only military casualty. Another one hundred and forty Indians were rounded up later along the cutbanks of the river where they had taken shelter. Of these, eighteen men were executed. One bullet to the back of the head. The others were released when word came from a scout who spotted the smoke from Mountain Chief's campfires several miles north along the same river.

Without food or adequate clothing, the remaining Peigan were forced to trek ninety miles to Fort Benton. The majority froze to death on the way there. Their feet black and blistered from frostbite.

Back at the Marias, Major Baker ordered his troops to set a funeral pyre for the bodies, and had his men round up the errant mustang ponies. He had ordered a second raid at dawn the next morning, but by then Mountain Chief's renegades had slipped across the Canadian border. They would never be caught.

The year of Wyoming's birth—1881—is an auspicious, or an inauspicious, one depending on how you look at it. The headlines screaming "Billy the Kid's Escape and Death" were hardly dry when news from the OK Corral broke in Tombstone, Arizona. Wyatt Earp, the infamous buffalo hunter, stagecoach driver, and sometime peace officer, lead his brothers Virgil and Morgan, as well as their friend Doc Holliday, the tubercular dentist, on a collision course with destiny that same October.

A set of random acts and chance encounters that fateful day, following months of mutual antagonism and animosity, landed the band in a standoff with Ike Clanton, his brother, and the McLaury boys. Sandwiched in an alley between Fly's Photography Studio and the private home of the Harwood family, no more than twenty feet apart, there came a showdown between cowboy and the Eastern establishment, rustler and lawman—the Old West and the New.

Reports have it that Billy and Frank McLaury drew first. Virgil—the town marshal—ordered them to throw down. But the men could see the writing on the wall. If the showdown wasn't today, it would only be another some time down the road. Under Doc Holliday's flapping coattails they could clearly see a shotgun, and Wyatt had a reputation all his own.

"Sonovabitch!" one of the men called, and then the shots rang out.

Wyatt did not flinch as bullets from Billy Clanton's gun flew past him and into the wall of Fly's Photography. He drew instead and put a slug in Frank McLaury's stomach. Morgan protected his older brother by hitting Billy through the wrist and once in the chest. The force of the second shot put him through a window of the Harwood house. But when he recovered, he only switched to his left hand and kept on firing.

Ike Clanton, the toughest talker of the crowd, refused to draw, and only lunged at Wyatt, who pushed him away. Doc levelled the shotgun beneath his coat at Tom McLaury and sent him staggering backward into the dust. Tom crawled and walked a half block before dying in the road.

Virgil was the first of the Earps to be hit. Billy Clanton put a bullet through his calf, though the lawman had not even drawn his weapon at that point. Frank McLaury stumbled into the main street trying to retrieve a shotgun from the saddle of his startled horse. He was leaking like a rain barrel. When the horse broke free, he was left to face Doc Holliday, who dropped the clumsy shotgun he used to kill Tom McLaury and drew his own pistol.

Frank fired first and Doc returned a split second later at the same time as Morgan Earp fired from the alley. Morgan's bullet entered Frank's ear and felled him in a heap. When the smoke cleared, Doc too was down in the street.

Eight men took part in a gunfight lasting only thirty seconds. Three men died. Three others were wounded. Wyatt and Ike came through without a scratch.

In that fine line between lawman and outlaw, the Earps were tried and found innocent. Thirty seconds and the myth grew.

After Butch destroyed the express car on the Overland Flyer, Wyoming thought they had all been killed. Their torsos, their arms, and their legs, even their faces, were covered in blood. The surrounding trees were marked as well. Wyoming searched his body in the first seconds after the explosion for the source of the leak. But he could find no wound.

And so he looked to the man next to him, who was looking back at him with the same confused expression. When each was satisfied that the blood did not belong to him, nor to the man standing closest, he began to examine those further afoot. But the entire gang seemed unharmed. Even Woodcock, the unfortunate rail guard, seemed to be intact.

Sundance was the first to laugh. And slowly each man turned to watch as he cleaned the substance off his finger with the help of his tongue.

"Raspberries," he grinned. And soon Butch joined him. Laughter rolling in like a storm. They were all like children then, grinning and slapping each other on the back.

When Wyoming remembers this, he is aware that it was not that funny. But the laughter then had been more like a collective sigh. A physical expression of their relief to know that they were still alive. That they had somehow come back from the dead.

Wyoming takes an axe down to the water. The river is little more than a stream now. A trickle of stone and silt. A small grove of pine stand amongst struggling cottonwood. Half drowned in the mud. High waters have washed away part of the fencing in Veccha's pasture. He is here to cut poles for the mending. His boots slap wet into earth as he sets himself for the first swing. His arms are weak with the days of inactivity. The axe cleaves mute into trunk.

He has lost precious time in tarrying here. But in some ways, it is as though time does not move here at all. Not in the way he is used to its calculation. Or perhaps it is just that days and weeks and months mean nothing to the millennia of a river cutting through prairie. But it is more difficult than that now. He has been seen.

The first tree falls and Wyoming moves on to the next, establishing a rhythm—the axe blade singing out two-four time. When the fourth tree breaks free of its roots, he is aware of a dull ache in his shoulder. But he works through the pain. Each cut exploding against the flesh of the tree, lulling him into the half-sleep of repetitive labour. When the task becomes reflex. Part of his being.

Now that he is well, he cannot stay. He must move north and lose himself in the ranches around Calgary. His presence here is a danger to Veccha. But he owes her this much at least. For food and for lodging. He watched her in the barn this morning. Bent over the milk pail, squeezing the warm fluid through her fingers. Her dress pulled tight over broad hips. The heavy swing of her breasts. Head leaning into the animal heat of the cow's belly, and strands of stray hair stuck to the side of her face with perspiration. He has never lived in such close proximity to a woman. Never experienced lust in domesticity. His mind is scrambled by it. A feeling like no other.

In under two hours, he has felled enough wood for a reserve of fence posts. When I have done this for her, I will leave, he says to himself. And he sets to clearing the branches and measuring off the appropriate lengths.

The Peigan way of life was one with the buffalo. Two Bears could ride and shoot before he could walk. The men in his world were called the All Comrades. A society organized around the hunt. They were grouped according to their age in clans like the Doves, the Flies, the All Brave Dogs, the Raven Bearers, the Catchers, and the Bulls. Each had its own role to play in relation to the buffalo herds.

They built their homes from the tanned hide of the buffalo. They used its fur to make winter coats and blankets. They burnt its bones to extract marrow. And it was their primary means of trade—at first with the Cree and the Shoshone, and eventually with the white man himself.

In the earliest days—before the bow and arrow, and long before the white man's horse—in the days of the atlatl and the spear—his people would drive the buffalo mad and frothing toward cliffs and coulee walls. Unable to stop, they would careen over the edge of these "jumps" and shatter themselves on the earth below. And in areas where there were no cliffs, the Peigan used buffalo pounds. Corrals of brush and hide into which they would drive small herds. And having them captive, they might slaughter them at close range. This is the way Napiw taught the first men to hunt.

But even Two Bears does not remember this way in his lifetime. He learned to hunt from a horse with bow and arrow. And eventually he was given a Springfield rifle. But no matter the innovation, his people hunted to live, and lived to hunt. The coming of the white man changed all that.

The white man did not love the buffalo as the Peigan did. They wanted only its hide. With their gifts and their tools they seduced many of the plains Indians, including the Peigan. And the over-hunting began. But nothing could match the devastation of the white hunter himself.

He rode into the plains on his iron horse when Two Bears was a young man. Before he had this demon horse that spit fire and smoke, the white man needed the Peigan to cull his furs. But now he came in large numbers and flooded the prairies with the scent of his killing. Two Bears and his brothers could ride for a day and not escape the wake of his passage. Fields of naked buffalo left to rot in the sun. The circling vultures blackened the sky.

He understood the elders' warnings then. He could see the future they predicted. One day the buffalo would be gone. And his people with it.

Veccha holds the newly shaped posts in place as Wyoming pounds them in with the sledge. He has removed his shirt. It is late afternoon. His muscles are oiled with the sweat of his labour and a fine layer of prairie washed over his skin.

He is beautiful, she thinks. And the sledge rolls over his shoulder, striking the post in her grip. They have almost completed the missing line of fence. Sinking the posts. One by one. Securing the rails with crossbeams. Tiny tipis. There has been no talk of his leaving.

She is surprised at the speed and ease with which he has insinuated himself into her life. Blown open the private world of her own construction. How effortlessly he moves in the world. How random.

He does not speak when he works. The labour transforms him. Channels the electrical pulse. The overabundance of synapse. Veccha helps him slot the final rails into place. Wyoming stands back, staring up and down the line of their work. Stretching back toward the cabin in linear perspective. His

body is spent. And just like that, Veccha is falling. Twisting palaeolithic through rivers of stone. Layers of rock and time. Her
nerves hum like telegraph wires collecting the unsolicited message. The vision.

Now she understands everything.

Wyoming is oblivious.

In the end, it was a grass fire, and not the white man, that drove
the buffalo away. The herds were already shrunken. Two thirds of
the Peigan were gone as well. Many killed by the white man's
sickness and whiskey. Others simply went hungry. But it was a
great conflagration west of the Cypress Hills that drove the
remaining herds south to Montana in search of food. They did
not return. And so the last of the free Indians went quietly to
their reservations—their dwindled barren lands—to subsist off
the white man's charity. But not Two Bears. Not his brothers.
Not as long as there were elk and deer. Not as long as there was a
rabbit to be taken. They would hold out through the first wave of
settlers, and the second. They would watch the Northwest
Mounted Police swoop in and mop up the whiskey posts.

They would remain to look after the sacred ground of their
ancestors. Until the last gathering in Two Bears's vision. They
would remain until the coming of the white boy to the prairie.

Each time Veccha asks him about Butch Cassidy, Wyoming ends
up in a story. He cannot find the words to encapsulate the man,
and so he allows the action of a good yarn to fill in the picture.
He tells her on one occasion about a robbery Butch committed
with Elzy Lay and Matt Warner. How the three bandits held up a
merchant carting wares between Vernal and Rock Springs.

Among the load of blankets and other household items, they

discovered several packages destined for a burlesque house in Louisiana. The majority of farmers in Brown's Park would never have laid eyes on the like, so Butch carted the otherwise useless load clear back to Utah. Once there, he gave them to a store-keeper by the name of John Jarvie, so that he might distribute the oddities fairly amongst the local population. He then left express instructions that the clothes and trinkets were to be worn at a dance the following Friday.

Wyoming describes to Veccha the spectacle of men in fishnet hosiery and housewives in ostrich feather boas of crimson and pink.

He exclaims, "One old fella shows up in a crinoline skirt with heels to boot! And if that ain't enough, when he finally gets his-self out on the dance floor, it suddenly becomes all too clear that he ain't wearin' no underclothes, neither." Wyoming slaps his leg. "I do declare, Butch found that one a wee bit queer."

Wyoming pokes among the files and the rock hammers on the workbench until he comes across something interesting, an arrowhead fashioned from stone. Upon closer investigation, he sees that there are several different projectiles of varying sizes and shapes.

"That is the head of an adze," Veccha says from the doorway. She proceeds to the table and carefully lays down the eggs she has gathered in her apron.

"It was a primitive axe. They attached it to a length of wood, like this." She simulates the construction with her hands. "Before the Europeans provided the plains Indian with steel, they were skilled stonesmiths."

Wyoming holds up an irregular-shaped rock larger than the others. "What's this?"

"That is a hammerstone. Two Bears gave it to me."

"What do you do with it?"

"Shape other stones. The Indians were always in search of a sharper edge. They used this to flake off and chisel other types of stone, like flint and quartzite. Those stones split like glass." Veccha reaches for the original arrowhead Wyoming discovered.

"This is obsidian. It can't even be found here naturally. It proves the Indians had regular trade routes to the south. This is most likely more than a thousand years old."

Wyoming can hardly imagine such a date. He has a difficult time thinking outside the moment.

"Let me show you how it is done." Veccha grabs a small piece of unshaped quartz and strikes it with the hammerstone. A clean flake breaks away.

"Now you try," she says, extending the tools.

But when Wyoming strikes the stone, it snaps into three pieces.

"No. Like this." Veccha takes his hands in hers. Leans in close. Wyoming stares at the white flesh at her temples. The stray hairs damp with perspiration. He can sense her body tightening, and then she releases his wrists too quickly.

"In any case, it is a delicate process," she says. And then she leaves the room.

Wyoming can still feel the warm stamp of her hands on his arms. The door gapes in her wake. Through the crack, he can just make out the white wash of her disappearing body.

At a ranch outside Lewistown Webb stops to rest his horse. The granger is nervous and overly attentive. Trying to engage Webb in conversation. Rain falls around them in big fat drops. The plateau stretches out around them like a drum. Plum bushes and stunted willows.

The rancher says, "Rain's been steady for more'n a week now."

But Webb is trying to ignore him. Something about the man has set him off. He wanders in the direction of the corral. Right now Sirango will be briefing the press, he thinks. Letting them know he is following up every lead. That he is close. So close. But Webb knows that behind the man's polished veneer, the first seeds of doubt will already have been sown. Pushing toward the surface. Tendrilling noiselessly beneath the man's pale skin.

"These all your plugs?"

The horses are equally nervous, rearing and packing before the oncoming storm. Webb must beat this man. Every man that has ever diminished him. Every woman.

"Yep. Took 'em half wild this spring," the man answers. "Say, would you like a drop a somethin'? Might even have some johnny-cake left over from dinner. Have to ask the missus."

Webb does not answer. Leans over the fence for a closer look. A big blue roan in his eye. More than a few fine horses prance and push about the yard, but nothing out of the ordinary. Then he sees it. First on the blue roan, then on a small pinto. Soon they're like beacons. Six all told.

"That brand," Webb says to no one in particular.

"What's that?"

"They ain't your horses," Webb turns with a smile. "Got somethin' to tell me?" And suddenly Sirango seems very small. Very far away.

Veccha wonders even now if her father moved the family to save her from this. A life of foretelling the future. Perhaps he thought new surroundings were enough to begin again without cultural baggage. But, of course, that would not have been enough. Nothing ever is. People. All people have a certain sixth sense of their own. They sense difference like they notice a new wrinkle in the face of a friend. And that is the way it has always been for Veccha.

No matter how far she strays from home. From the resting place of her mother.

It is odd, she thinks, that the two women never discussed their shared condition. Never commiserated. Her mother was still a young woman when she died. Perhaps she intended to address it at some later date. But of course, she would have known that that date would never arrive.

Veccha remembers her mother's hands more than any other feature. More than her eyes, even. Which were like Veccha's. For although sorrow can be found in the eyes well enough, it resides primarily in the hands. The way they lie folded in a lap. The way they curl into the warmth of a cup. They way they do not reach out to touch, or to love.

In the end, there are many reasons her father might have elected to leave Norway, she thinks. Why would he stop at just one?

Veccha has a splinter in her foot. She sits at the rail table examining the damage, prodding the toughened flesh. She does not see Wyoming as he leans in the doorway like a barn owl, with his shoulders tossed forward and collapsed around his chest. The air is still and the bleached ends of his lashes are the only things that move, beating the semi-dark of the cabin like the broken wings of a sparrow. And when she does finally become aware of his presence, it is a sensual experience, like fear or excitement. The small hairs on the exposed nape of her neck rise in response. Her breath quickens.

This is what it is like to be a fieldmouse, she thinks. And part of her shrinks away from the gaze. Sends signals through her bloodstream. The Morse code for terror. But there is another code beneath the first. Less alarming, but more insistent. Singing along the hidden corridors of her anatomy like a familiar ghost.

If he moves now, she thinks. If he comes to me as I sit here.

Veccha closes her eyes, and the world is a green afterimage. And even though his body is leaving the gravity of the doorway, she can hold him there like a memory until time erases his shadow. And then suddenly she is aware of his breath, his lips on the pad of her foot. When she opens her eyes, there is no balance to the room. Wyoming is kneeling before her. Blond hairs blooming like brush beneath the brim of his hat. When he looks up from the wound, a small wooden shard is trapped in the grip of his smile.

Wyoming follows the river of leg with his hands. Pressing his fingers into the round muscle of calf. The cave at the back of her knee. The wide expanse of thigh. He is crouching on the hard floor, looking up through the dust motes that spill over her shoulders. The halo of light in her hair. He can hear the shrill cry of a warbler in the yard, and his heart as it batters the ribs of its cage like a bird. A bee floats lazily through the room, unseen, and behind its buzz, the constant rusting creak of the windmill, drawing water from the earth.

His hands are black with the prairie, and they leave dark wakes of passage that disappear in the folds of her dress. Her ankle rests by his ear. The heel in his neck. The chair creaks as she opens herself to his touch. And when he reaches that place between her legs, her lips part in the middle of her face.

"Oh." The tongue like a plum.

Her foot twitches then, in reflex. His hat lands on the floor, and he allows himself to be reeled in like a fish, snapping and jerking. Her hands catch in his hair and draw his round face up to meet hers. Their warm tongues pass over the space between them. And the kitchen throbs like a heart.

A moment later, her hands have moved. The buttons of his trousers break over the hardwood floor and roll, searching out the corners of the room. Her dress tears at the breast. And he is inside her at once. When the legs of the chair split, and the wrangling couple spills over the floor, he does not leave her. Her arms flail out above her head, catching a leg of the table and an upturned bucket by the stove.

With one hand he lifts the heavy flesh of her hip. But there is no time to move. White heat rushes through his squirrelling pelvis. And he collapses over her like a fallen tree.

"Are you done?" she asks, after a short time has passed. The panting of his breath slowed.

He is staring at the bucket in her hand.

"Aren't you?"

They both laugh in the heat of the room.

Wyoming traces the passage of moonlight over the bed. The corridors of his mind are flooded with light. He has not slept. Unused to the body beside him. The landscape slumbering beneath sheets. It is the first time that he has spent the night with a woman. He feels small next to her. Not in any physical way. Though there is that. He is reminded instead of cattle drives on the open plateaux. Of grey mornings shot through with a lining of sun in the clouds. Days when the sky has a sense of texture and depth, enough to remind him of the grandeur of things and his insignificance within them.

But this is not a bad feeling. Rather it is one of reassurance. Of warmth. For no matter what he does, no matter how badly he messes up, something bigger than himself is always making sure that things go right. That his incompetence will be overlooked in the grand scheme of things. But he also feels somehow protected. Isolated from the evils of the world. For indeed, one is often alone in the big country of Wyoming. Even when surrounded by men, doing the same job. There is always something good and wholesome about riding so close to animals. Packing and snubbing. Feeling the warmth of their dumb bodies plodding anonymously over the long grass of the high plain.

Lying next to Veccha gives him the same sense of security. That same sense of communion with the world. As though both time and space have broken away from their human constraints and he is at one with all that has been. All that will be.

He is a small man grappling with big issues in the dark. And so he cannot sleep. Refuses to have this moment slip through his fingers like sand on the prairie. But underneath this impetus for stasis there is another nagging thought. An unwanted knock at the door.

He must leave this place. And Veccha. It cannot be otherwise. He is not at ease with decisions. And so he watches the moonlight for hours until the bed is swallowed in darkness.

The Winters trail is cold as a grave. Webb is more than two weeks late. And still it is raining. But there is something. A rumour. A joke. When Webb digs up the newspapers from Grand Falls, the story is confirmed. A botched robbery in Havre. It is more than he hoped for. Besides, Webb's mind does not work that way. Does not understand hope. He runs on absolutes. This is what he is looking for. The key through the next door.

He can hear the soft tongues of the newspapermen as they wag after Sirango, two thousand miles away. Already they will be whispering among themselves. "Gone." "Escaped." They will have begun to see through the man's talk. The flippant self-assurance. The starched collar, too white. And although he does not smile at this, Webb is pleased. He still has the scent like a dog.

It is not Curry. Of this he is sure. The job is too sloppy. No one is killed in the escape. Not a single shot even fired. But there are other possibilities. He rides north again. Sniffing. Sniffing. Storm clouds racing behind.

When Wyoming is not working, he is talking. Telling stories like someone else might sneeze. He speaks in an awkward drawl. Drawing out vowels, producing syllables where previously there were none. And through all this Veccha listens and is entertained. She cannot remember a time when she was as happy. Suppressing the vision. The new dream she has found.

"Butch once held a Thanksgiving feast for the ranchers of Brown's Park. He invited all the local residents and their wives out to the Davenport Ranch. Thirty-five people all told. Kinda like a thank-you party."

"For what did he thank them?"

"Well, ya see. Butch had a theory. A lot of them actually. He thought if he threw a little money around, helped people out, that they'd be more inclined to hide him out or to do him a good turn if the law ever came lookin'. So Butch used his share of the earnings from the Wilcox train robbery to have a big meal cooked for the community.

"He served up blue point cocktails with roast turkey and chestnut dressing. He even had cranberries doled out on the side. And Roquefort cheese, straight from France. Though I didn't eat none a that. And for dessert, there was pumpkin pie.

"Funniest thing about it, though? Butch is worse than a mother hen. He got to worryin' so much about doin' things proper, he done made hisself sick. When it came time to serve tea, his nerves was so shot, he couldn't pour straight. Got to thinkin' that maybe there was a right way to pour tea and he didn't know it. This is the same guy what plays around with explosives for a living. Anyway, we end up in the kitchen—Butch and Sundance and me—havin' him practise the proper pour and showin' him how you raise your pinky finger like so."

Wyoming stands in the middle of the room, modelling the ideal tea-drinking stance. Batting his lashes and slurping audibly.

When Veccha stops laughing, she knots her brow as though considering something of great importance. "Your stories are always about men. Are there any women on the American prairie? Were there no lovers?"

Wyoming considers this a moment. Twisting his lips as he concentrates. Coming down from the rush of storytelling. Slowing. His eyes lower before he speaks.

"Well, there was Etta."

"Who?"

"Etta Place. I don't know if that was her proper name. But that's what we called her. She was there at Thanksgiving. Sundance was sweet on her. And she knew it too. They was like pork and beans, them two."

"Was she beautiful?"

"She wasn't like the others. Not like Laura Bullion, who was one of us. Not like Lillie Davis. She was a schoolteacher. Or so I heard. Never saw her do much teachin'. But she was fine. A lady. So I believe it. She was cultured, like. Fact is, she was so smart I could never stick two words together when she was around. She hadda way of lookin' at ya. Like she was lookin' straight through, ya know?"

"And what about Butch? Didn't he have a girl?"

"I reckon' there were a few. Here and there. None in particular. He liked Etta well enough, I guess. I think it ett him up some that she was with the Kid."

"And did she like Butch as well?"

Wyoming must think long about this question.

"I think maybe she loved them both," he responds, as though this is some sort of revelation. "Or maybe not. I dunno. Think that's strange? Lovin' two men at the same time? Is that possible?"

Veccha does not answer immediately. The sun has time to chart its course across the floor an inch.

"This is not so strange, I think."

Of course there were women in the West. And more specifically, there were women on the Outlaw Trail. But the women Wyoming was most accustomed to greeting were of the professional sort, and he was sure that Veccha was not enquiring after them. But the truth about women in the West was that they were in short supply. A cowboy might ride one hundred miles just to court the closest available woman. One hundred miles to sip lemonade on the front porch of a father's house. And then he might go months before seeing her again, dependent upon the distance of his seasonal drive, or the welcome of that same father.

But among the working women and the delicate desert flowers of the West, there was another breed of woman, tough as nails and just as hard as any man. Women like Annie Oakley, Belle Starr, Charley Parkhurst, and Cattle Kate. Women who defied presiding social convention and made a name for themselves as cowgirls, rustlers, markswomen, and stagecoach drivers. But, perhaps no other woman is so definitive in her embodiment of that conquering frontier spirit as Calamity Jane.

Born in 1852, a full twenty-nine years before Wyoming, Marthy Burke—better known as Calamity Jane—forewent traditional women's clothing for most of her life, and actually soldiered alongside General Armstrong Custer as a scout during an early Indian campaign in Arizona. Her military career would later take her into such infamous skirmishes as the Nez Perce outbreak along the Musselshell in 1872, and into close contact with Lakota warriors in the Black Hills while protecting European miners. She was even stationed at Laramie in 1875. And although she had the good fortune not to be with Custer in 1876, she had joined other forces along the Big Horn River.

As destiny would have it, Jane met Wild Bill Hickok in Laramie shortly thereafter and decided to leave the military. She accompanied him to Deadwood instead, where she entered the ranks of the Pony Express and rode with them for a summer over one of the most dangerous trails in the West. The fifty-mile stretch between Deadwood and Custer. She managed to complete the route safely on numerous occasions, but returned to Deadwood on August 2nd, 1878, to the news that Hickok had been shot dead by John McCall. It was she who cornered him with a butcher knife shortly after, precipitating his initial arrest. Jane returned to the military for several years after, but eventually married and retired to a ranch with her husband. Like many bright stars during that period of history, she faded with the closing of the West, but her name lived on long after her.

Veccha remembers growing up as the only woman in a house of men. She has seen her older brothers naked. Many times. By accident and by device. She can still recall their long slim bodies stripped bare at the river. Unabashed and proud. The small gardens of hair on their pubis. The virile swing of their sex as they ran to the water. And she can also remember her own modest plodding at the same river. Separated by reeds. Wading in her own private pool. Never dreaming that she would remove the underclothes between her and the water.

Robert too had a body to which she was privy. And yet she is somehow unprepared for Wyoming. The constant sight of his buttocks. His naked walks around the room as he tells her stories. His penis dangling like a fruit.

Wyoming walks along the pitch of the barn roof because he can. No other reason than that. Veccha is anxious. Shouts to him once.

"Come down from there." And places her hands on her hips afterwards. Sets her jaw against his will.

But he only chuckles at the tantrum. Continues to strut like a rooster. Spinning on the balls of his feet when he reaches the edge. Strolling back in the other direction.

"Why do you do this?" she calls to him.

"Are ya scairt?" he replies. Not processing the change in her voice.

"Come down," she orders a second time.

And now he is laughing out loud. Touches down with one hand to steady himself. The sky is crystal azure. Has been that way for days. Long before his arrival. The horizon is a baker's oven, wobbling with heat. Evaporating before his eyes.

"Watch this," he calls back to her. Sets his feet and turns cartwheels all the way across the peak, until he is no longer sure which way is up. When he comes to a rest at the edge, the world keeps turning. But Veccha is gone. He can hear her sobbing inside the cabin.

Veccha tells Wyoming about Robert. Because he does not ask. She is not accustomed to telling stories about the past. She trades in the future. It is late. They are naked beneath the blankets. Staring out the window at stars.

"He was a man of science. Of empirical evidence. He studied the logic of lost people. Like the early aboriginals of Australia. The Siksika and the Shoshone of Milk River. He showed me how to read hieroglyphics. The declarations of pharaohs. I met him on my father's farm in Foremost. He stayed with us because we had room. There are no hotels outside Lethbridge.

"He was working for the Royal Geographical Society of Britain. *Asinipai'pi*, a place of stories, was to be his great discovery. His field of study. He was determined to become famous. Like Livingston, perhaps. The prairie was to be his undiscovered country. But he was not meant to live in this world.

"My father warned me not to marry this man. He will not survive the winter, he told me. And my father was correct. But it was not the prairie winds that took him. He is buried in South Africa.

"He squandered the grant money on supplies. Everything had to be shipped in from Vancouver or ferried overland from Toronto. Montreal. He was a man of pride. Could not turn to my family for help. So he joined his English king in a war against the Boer. He joined him for a paycheque."

"Did you ... did you see his death?"

"Like a rainbow."

"But hadn't you dreamt of him since childhood?"

"I was mistaken."

At twenty yards, Wyoming can hit small animals on the run. Tin cans go off like rockets, remain airborne long enough for two more shots. The satisfying pop. This is a trick he has learnt from Sundance and Carver. Something to perform at parties. But beyond this is an ocean. The horizon, blue blur. Trees disappear in the pool of his eyes.

He has learned to hide his nearsightedness. He is studied in the art of unconscious compensation. Like a blind man, he has developed a keen sense of smell. Ears like a jackrabbit. In his profession, weakness means certain death. There is no honour among thieves. Hens at a pecking party.

And so to Veccha, he is a hawk coughing bullets. Picking off tin cans at the edge of his visible world. Making it look easy. The consummate actor.

"Two hundred million years ago, this valley was an ocean. And the birds were fish."

They are sitting by the river, hidden by thickets, when she tells him this. They have just made love.

"Before the ice came, this land was ancient and flat. Unravaged by time. It was the consequence of a billion years of sediment piled at the bottom of the sea. Animal bones and plant life. All this is new," she says. Waving her arms. Encompassing the coulee with its strangled cottonwoods and isolated willow. A world of wild grass and knotted rush.

Only now, as Veccha serves it up to him like an offering, can Wyoming pick out the individual song of frog and lark and bee. The sweet-grass scent of algae.

"The Great Plains owe their features to ice. That came much later. Once the waters were gone. When the glaciers withdrew, like the waters before them, they left scars on the prairie. Moraines. Lake basins. Deltas and spillways. This valley is glacially contorted bedrock left open to the wind.

"Someday this too will be gone. The rock art. The medicine wheels. And the process will begin again."

"Do you think we'll be here the next time around?" he asks with a grin. Staring up at the sky.

"I know it," she says.

And the boy laughs. Pleased with her first attempt at humour.

That afternoon she takes him to the medicine wheel. Robert uncovered it only weeks before he left. It lies atop a low-grade hill in the high prairie. The grass that her husband had previously cleared has regrown now, but the structure is still visible. A double ring defined by several hundred stones. Each too large for one man to carry. Its central cairn is several metres wide and almost as tall as a man. To reach it, they follow a path, clearly marked with smaller stones, two parallel lines pulling them into the inner circle. This is her favourite place, she tells the boy. She is strongest here. And it is no coincidence that this is the first site she shows him. Since Wyoming's arrival, her dreams have been frightening. She is hoping for a sign. A gift from the stones.

"Robert told me it was the Oxbow people who built this site.

They came here from the east, beyond the Cypress Hills, more than five thousand years ago. That's almost one thousand years before Stonehenge."

Wyoming stands at arm's length from the altar. Spins away on the heel of his boot. Taking in the size of the thing.

"There are others," she continues. "But not like this one. The double ring sets it apart. Some are shaped like wagon wheels with spokes emanating from a fixed point in the earth. Robert saw one once in the form of a tree. But most are single-ring circles. Unbroken by lines, with a central stone. From the sky, they must look like a great unblinking eye."

"But what are they? What do they ... do?"

Veccha pauses a moment, considering.

"It is impossible to know for sure, but Robert has suggested that they were ceremonial in nature. Used for religious rites, perhaps. He found remnants of trade goods, arrowheads, and obsidian at the base of the central cairn. He says that they were offerings."

Wyoming looks at the great stone sticking up from the earth like a thumb.

"But what do you think?" he asks her.

The question comes like an unexpected letter, and Veccha must take a moment longer.

"I think that they represent the universe," she stumbles. Never having had the need to verbalize what she knows. What she feels to be true. "The circles. The continuity of things." She pauses again, at a loss for words.

Wyoming waits patiently. Hands at his sides.

"Don't you hear it?" she manages finally.

He frowns. "Hear what?"

"The whispers. I think they're like secrets."

That night, there is a new dream swimming through the rivers of her mind. A cool fish flitting elusive. Thrashing like madness. It is a violent dream. Cold as a metaphor. She is not sure that she wishes its capture, if it has anything to do with the recent vision. Just this once, she is begging for mystery, the option to discover by chance.

But she is her mother's daughter. And her minds whips on in the wake of the fish until she can see the individual scales, flashing like blood. The fear in its eyes, clear as a catastrophe. And she knows immediately that she will forevermore measure time as before and after this moment.

Although she would never think of herself as their equal, Veccha believes that she has some understanding of the heavy burden carried by the Indian mystics who came before her. She feels a particular kinship with the Lakota leader, Sitting Bull, who came through *Asinipai'pi* on his way to the Land of the Grandmother. He was plagued even then by the weight of his visions. Veccha gathered his story from Two Bears and the rumour of popular legend. But in some deeper way she had always known it.

It is said that in 1872, during a gun battle with US troops, Sitting Bull and four other mystics walked out into the field between the warring factions, sat down, and smoked their pipes. When they were through, the men stood up and walked back to their tents, unharmed. Sitting Bull foresaw the early victories of his people at Rosebud Creek. And again in a famous vision that showed him soldiers riding upside down and falling into an Indian village, he predicted their success at Little Bighorn.

How, though, she wonders, would he have delivered the subsequent visions? The foreshadowing of a people's demise? How would he have told his wife or his children that his own people would come for him someday? That he would die at their hands?

The slave race of a once-proud nation. Perhaps if she knew the answers to these questions, she would be better able to deal with her latest visions and the pathway blazed in her dreams.

Webb makes a deal with the river. With the rain. Today is the low point in his journey. He cannot shake the weather. There is a fever in his eyes. His mind is a sponge. It is dark and he is still a half day from Havre, longer if he cannot manage the ford. He urges the reluctant stallion into the torrent. The water swells to his belly.

Webb has been thinking of Rose. All day her image like a hot poker in his ear. The milky white skin on the small of her back. If only the rain would stop, he could think clearly. But it is part of him now. Essential to the story.

The waters rise up over the withers and then the horse is swimming. Being carried downstream. Snorting and crying. Webb still cannot focus. But there are instincts as old as the river, screaming through his nervous system. Forcing him to resist. He pulls the horse back into position like a sleepwalker. Urges him forward. The animal panting hard now. Struck dumb with fright. And then one hoof strikes river bottom. Half floating and walking, it struggles through loose stone and shale.

On the far shore, nothing but rain is there to greet him. And still all he can think of is Rose. The heat in his head like a driven nail.

The next day she takes him to the wall. They walk through the high grass, tempered by wildflowers and lady's slipper, growing crowded in the flood plain of the Milk River. Hawks float in the wind above their heads. Spinning eastward like water through a pulled plug. It is a silent journey.

The coulee wall is the only geographical formation of any

significance on the prairie, aside from the wizened hoodoos to the south. It is the product of downcutting and a million years of wind. So dominant in this landscape that it is visible from a great distance. When up close, it is difficult for a person to remain unmoved by the proximity of its solid sandstone face, stretching east and west like a set of grim teeth.

"Look," she tells him, pointing out the layers of stratification. "You can see backward in time. Farmers have dug up dinosaur bones in their fields to the north. Imagine how far back we are here."

Wyoming reaches out to the wall with his hands. The way Veccha did a year ago. The same reaction.

"Here is an earthquake. Like a million-year-old signature. Here is the resting place of a leaf. A fish from the Eocene."

She shows the boy a number of geological events. Increments of time. And the knowledge she holds out to him soaks through his skin. Finally, she leads him to her husband's favourite site. The arrival of man.

"Here is the history of a great war. Those round shield figures are three thousand years old. They're called petroglyphs. Etchings in stone."

"There is a horse here." Wyoming points to a depression in the wall.

"Yes. This is a new marking. No more than two hundred years old."

"How can you tell?"

"Europeans introduced the horse to the plains. This is a ceremonial hunt. Notice the flowing headdress like a veil? These are called pictographs. Painted in ochre. Iron ore mixed with water."

"Picture books," Wyoming exclaims.

"Yes," Veccha answers. "Picture books. The Siksika call this place *Asinipai'pi*—'it has been written.' They arrived in this valley five hundred years ago. The earliest carvings were done by the

Shoshone, the Kutenai, and the Atsina. It was a place of great power in all their cultures. It still is."

Veccha takes him from site to site, revealing the mysteries of this underground cathedral—heraldic shields, sunbursts, and cryptic lines.

"Where did the natives go?"

"There is no evidence that they ever lived here. A few tipi rings on the outer edge of the wall. This is sacred ground. This is where they buried their dead. Recorded their stories."

"Do they use it still?"

"No. The Peigan were the last to leave. They disappeared with the bison."

Veccha considers the persistence of Two Bears. But she has not seen him since the boy's arrival. Perhaps he too has left the valley forever, she thinks. Which would make her cabin the last outpost.

"I wish we wrote like this. With pictures. This is the first book I ever read."

"You cannot read?"

Wyoming blushes. Kicks the dust with his oversized boot.

"But your books . . ." she begins, and soon understands. "Come. I will teach you."

She extends her hand like a branch.

In a world of semi-literate outlaws, the gun was as good as a signature. Samuel Colt saw to that.

At the tender age of sixteen, on his way to India as a cabin boy on a merchant ship, he carved what was to be a model for his first infamous "six-shooter." A pistol with a rotating cylinder that allowed the gunman to fire six shots before reloading—revolutionary in a world where handguns were previously reloaded after only one discharge. And a marvel for the American military during the Mexican and Civil wars.

The West's most feared killer, John Wesley Hardin, touted a black early model .38-.40 calibre Colt with cap and ball shot. And it was Billy the Kid who made the .41 calibre "self-cocking" Colt Thunderer famous. His particular piece had a lovely bird's-head grip inlaid with bone. But it wasn't just the outlaws who put their faith in Colt. A number of dubious lawmen carried the very same sidearms. Wild Bill Hickok, for instance, swore by the then old-fashioned 1851 Navy Colt Single Action Conversion. In fact, he made it a habit to carry two of them for increased comfort. And Wyatt Earp was known to brandish a unique version of the .45 calibre single-action Colt Buntline Special, with a sixteen-inch barrel for increased accuracy, even if it was a little clumsy off the draw. But no one loved his guns like the card sharp Doc Holliday, who took a number of lives with his .38 calibre Colt Lightning. Although it was also rumoured that he kept a .41 calibre over-and-under nickel-plated Derringer up his sleeve, just in case.

But if Colt reigned supreme, there were, nonetheless, a few pretenders to the throne kicking around as well. Jesse James, for instance, preferred the firepower of his .45 calibre Smith & Wesson Schofield, while his brother pledged allegiance to anything made by Remington. And in an interesting turn of events, the cowardly Bob Ford posed for a photograph, after killing Jesse, carrying the pearl-handled .44 calibre Smith & Wesson American that same outlaw gave him years earlier as a gift. Even Wyoming bucked the Colt trend, preferring instead to stick with his father's .44 calibre Remington New Model Army.

It's almost a bit overwhelming to consider the variety of models, conversions, and even decorative possibilities available to the gunman in that violent time—like the silver-plated, scroll-engraved .44 calibre Smith & Wesson with ivory grip, or the .45 calibre Eagle Butt Peacemaker with embossed mother-of-pearl. But then men will do almost anything to leave their mark on the world.

They begin with the alphabet and move on to his name. Wyoming's tongue does most of the work. Tracing the letters in the air above the page as though guiding his unwilling hand.

It is night. The lantern burns a bubble around them, fends off darkness and the last collapse of day. The muscles that feed his fingers and the tendons in the back of his arm are knotted and sore. He copies the model she has created for him—Ewen McGinnis. In fine flowing cursive. But try as he might, his own efforts appear childish and raw. The loops are misshapen and large. The vertical lines, crooked and halting. Lacking in unity, the letters work against themselves, like a graveyard of tipped and crooked stones.

But he is a dedicated pupil. He struggles long into the night. Even after Veccha falls asleep at the table. Necessity is the mother of invention.

Sometimes he will awake in the middle of the night and already be inside her. Drawn unconsciously like a compass needle to a lodestone. These are the moments when he cannot believe his luck. This. After hours of lovemaking already. Her body moving, responding. Still half asleep and yearning. Somnolent fucking. The pure evolutionary urge.

Two Bears arrives while they are still in bed. His rap at the door is a singular burst. Veccha throws a dress over her head quickly. She does not put up her hair. When she opens the door, the sunlight is new to her eyes. Makes her squint for recognition. She has lost track of the days, and so she is expecting perhaps the seekers. It is the first time that she has seen Two Bears without his horse. She is surprised to find that he is not a tall man. His brothers remain by the gate. Visible over his shoulders. Solemn as gravestones.

Wyoming appears in the background wearing only his pants.

Two Bears acknowledges the boy with a nod, as though his presence were not unusual. The Peigan is dressed in full regalia. The headdress of feather and bone. The beaded breastplate. The trappings of his ancestors. This too is new. Veccha slides into the foreign tongue with a little effort.

"Good morning. I have missed you."

Veccha is sure that she sees the man's face flush.

"We have been making preparations."

"Preparations for what?"

"The time has come. Napiw has spoken to me. We go north to join our families in Buffalo Jump."

"But who will watch over the burial grounds? The art?" Veccha is alarmed by the news. Her eyes dart over the small man's face, searching for answers. She plays nervously with the folds of her dress.

"You can't leave," is what she says. But *I don't want you to go* is what she is thinking.

"There is still much power here. We will come back some day, like all things. But our home is elsewhere now. You will be here when we are gone."

"But ... who ... who will look after me?"

Two Bears stares over her shoulder at the boy, who has remained quiet. In awe of the conversation. He straightens now. Aware that the talk has turned to him.

"You will be fine, I think."

Now it is Veccha's turn to blush.

"But do you go now?"

"No. We will perform the Sundance at the medicine wheel before we leave. When it has been done, we will depart."

"You will return to say goodbye?"

"You too will be leaving here soon, I think?" He relapses into a questioning deference. Only this time, there is also the hint of a suggestion in his voice. The push that she has been waiting for.

"I don't know," is all she can answer.

"We will perform the Sundance first," he repeats. "We shall all meet again."

Veccha watches the upright figure of Two Bears as he spins and lopes back to his horse. She knows that Wyoming will be staring too.

Sitting Bull spent the last years of his life on the Standing Rock Reservation in North Dakota. Chief Kicking Bear visited him there with news of a Paiute mystic named Wevoca. The young man predicted the resurrection of his people through a ceremony called the Ghost Dance. Kicking Bear had already experienced the power of the dance. He had seen Indian warriors collapsing into trance and tears. Wailing for the fate of their people. Confident that they would one day rise again.

What Kicking Bear wanted from the old Lakota was his confirmation of the Wevoca's vision. But Sitting Bull was no longer visited by dreams of his own. He would not comment on the Ghost Dance.

This is a story Two Bears relates to Veccha.

"I first danced the Ghost Dance when I was a child," he adds. "I have not danced it since. My people have long since ceased to believe. But I will see it danced again one day before I leave this place."

And she believed him.

Webb rocks into the woman beneath him, but thinks only of Rose. Of his ruined career. His failure to hunt down the thief. He pays two dollars to give away a part of himself to this stranger, lying lonely under the bulk of his body, because the rain has halted his progress. It pounds even now on the windowsill.

After questioning the members of each posse, he has nothing.

The trail ends at a brothel in Havre. He is drunk and a fever burns in his eyes. Butch Cassidy is gone. And Sundance is with him. They will surface years later in South America. Or maybe Australia. Both of them out of his reach.

When he looks in the eyes of the woman beneath him, he sees only himself. And realizes then he is crying. The girl is frightened, at first. Doing her best to look over his shoulder. But he is through. Rolls off her and out of the bed. She tries to speak to him then. To console him. Imagining perhaps a different sort of man. Confused by his display of emotion. And so she tells him a story in an effort to connect. To reach across the loneliness between them.

She tells him the miraculous story about the boy in her bedroom weeks earlier. And the woman. Alone on the prairie.

Wyoming leaves Veccha at the cabin. She is sleeping. Has been distraught all morning since the Indian left. And now, even as she sleeps, her rest is fraught with dreams. It is a long walk to the water in summer. The current has slowed to a crawl. He has taken the habit of swimming in the late afternoon before supper. It is an immaculate day. The banks of the river are bursting with wild bergamot, smooth aster, and milkweed. Flathead chub float listless near the water's surface, sunning themselves. And the air is fresh, predicting rain. Even the frogs call out for it in an unsurpassed chorus of peeping.

Beyond the sandstone wall of the coulee, Wyoming can see nothing—but he imagines the pale green silhouette of Montana's Sweetgrass Hills. A reminder of where he has come from and from what he is running.

Normally he is cheered by his trek to the river. Walking waist-high through bluestems and switchgrass. Brushing the tips of their growth with his fingers. Observing the nervous flit of meadowlarks, the long soaring path of the hawks. But the night before he learned to sign his name. An almost unintelligible scribble. He must face reality. Thirty thousand dollars in unsigned notes, and no hope of using them.

Wyoming has left a trail across the desert only a blind man could not follow. He finds himself anticipating the cold press of steel at the back of his head, and he realizes now that even Calgary is not safe. He is part of a dying breed. The cold fact Butch offered him the night before Wagner. When he reaches the water, he strips down to nothing. Sets his boots carefully amid sagebrush and thistle. The water is a lukewarm bath, running lazily over him. He picks it up in handfuls, splashing his face. Tossing it over his shoulders. Listening to its cool chant as it rolls back into the current. The river's unquenchable thirst for the sea. It will carry his scent back to the lawmen of Montana and eventually dump him into the Gulf of Mexico by way of the Missouri and the Mississippi. He has the urge to lie back and follow the river's meandering course. To give himself up to its pull.

A water moccasin slips from the edge of the bank.

He has not mentioned the money to Veccha. He did not dare in the beginning. And now it would be as though he harboured a secret. He looks back to the southern horizon. Expecting to see a dust cloud of detectives bearing down upon him.

There is a seed in his brain. Something Veccha said a few days ago about Robert's work in Australia. The same seed planted by Sundance and Butch. But he would need to cross the mountains to reach Vancouver. And for that he would need to steal a horse. There, he could maybe work a steamship. And Veccha?

He plunges headlong into the muddy waters. Holding his breath. Swimming upstream through patches of weed. When he surfaces—spitting and gasping for air—he has barely moved from the place he began.

The cabin door is open to him when he arrives. A fact he does not register. The last two weeks have taken the edge off his senses. A horse is tied in the yard as well. But it is hidden in the blur of his eyes. Were he not so involved in his thoughts, he might have recognized the smell. Picked up on the sound of its tail batting at flies. As it is, Wyoming is inside the dark room of the cabin before he can process any of this.

Veccha sits at the table. Her body is tilted away. But she looks to him over her shoulder. The broad, tanned face. Only after does he see Logan. Smiling like a jackal. A gun in his hand.

Instinct arrives before thought. The boy's revolver lies empty on the table between them. The space is too far to cover. He cannot lunge. And Veccha cuts off his only escape. She sits on the lap of the outlaw. That's when Wyoming notices the Montana peak perched on Logan's head like a joke. Constable Whitfield. Lying face up in the river now, and heading out to sea. Wyoming cannot run. Logan means business.

"You done staked yerself out a nice bit of territory, Ewen." Logan's free arm is wrapped around Veccha in a mocking embrace. The big paw of hand cupping her breast.

"She sure does smell nice."

An unrecognizable feeling swells up from within the boy. His throat constricts and he is aware, for the first time, of his ability to kill. Roused like a sleeping bear from its den.

"Logan" is the only sound he produces. But the hatred is palpable. It sticks to the word.

"Now. Don't do nothin' stupid, amigo." Logan waves the pistol in the air by his head as though he is waving goodbye. "I done looked through yer saddlebags. And you know what I found? Nothin'. That's what. I know you took the money, you fuckin' little Irish dwarf. It's the only reason I didn't shoot you in the doorway. Now where the fuck did you hide it?"

Wyoming has jumped from cliff faces onto the back of moving locomotives. He has been in gunfights after a heist. But now is the only time he has been aware of his own mortality. The pulsing vein above Logan's left eye is a sure sign that death awaits him this afternoon. Only he is not frightened. The knowledge is oddly liberating. A calm settles over his body. His shoulders relax and soon he finds himself smiling.

"Where's Kilpatrick?"

"Never you mind. I'm askin' the questions around here. And wipe that stupid smile off yer face. Are you fuckin' simple? Tell me where the fuckin' money is or I'll kill her here in the chair." Logan places the long cool barrel of the gun in the soft flesh around Veccha's temple. But her eyes betray no fear. She too is disturbingly calm. And it occurs to Wyoming that she might actually have foreseen Logan's act of intrusion. That they are living out an intricate dance. One where all the steps have been predetermined.

"I buried it," he answers.

"Don't play with me, Ewen. Where the fuck is it buried?"

"The medicine wheel. I'll have to show you. You'd never find it without me."

"Take that fuckin' shovel by the wall." Logan uses his pistol to point. "We can use it later to cover yer body."

Wyoming remembers only vaguely where the medicine wheel lies. And although he leads the tiny band over the stretch of prairie to the rock face, he must look often to Veccha for guidance. There is a certain degree of courage needed to accept what fate has laid out for you, Wyoming thinks, as they kick their way through the buffalo grass. To accept what you have already done, time and time again. For how else could one possibly know what the future holds, unless it has already happened?

Now and again Logan throws insults. Threatens Wyoming with all manner of torture as they become lost in the flatlands.

Things that would have set the boy off only yesterday. But he is released from this. If he were to have only one role—one fate—he would not choose Logan's. He would not reverse the circumstances that occur on this walk. That role would be unbearable. And suddenly the significance of his choice to lead the man out into the desert—to have concocted a plan to lie about the money—seems cosmically important. And his previous theory—his longing for the security of an anonymous life—seems like faulty logic. No one is looking out for Wyoming. Making sure things go right. The choice is his. A choice he has already made.

When he reaches what is obviously the medicine wheel, his mind is spinning. Stones are placed at specific intervals, like points on a compass. Some are larger than others. A few appear to be missing. Veccha is glowing. Her skin is radiant here at the centre of the wheel. Even Wyoming feels the power like an electrical current passing through his limbs.

"Well ... what are you waitin' for? Start digging, kid."

Wyoming is roused from his reverie by the sharp voice, like chain dragged over rock. He is not sure what he intended to take place. What good it was to bring the man here. But it seems like an unforgivable trespass to break the soil with the spade in his hands.

"You dig or she dies."

Wyoming places the shovel in a patch of dry earth. Perhaps the ancient remains of a firepit. But before the blade passes into the ground, he is stopped. Two Bears and his brothers materialize out of the prairie like ghosts from a fog. Each of them in the deerskin dress of his ancestors. Feathers and silverberry beads. Warbonnets and coup sticks. And then Wyoming realizes that they are surrounded by the Peigan. Willowy men with long flowing hair. Women clutching their children.

Logan tosses his head from one face to another. And back to Wyoming for an explanation. But the boy's face is a mirror. Logan's eyes flicker like small candles. And then he stumbles backward, releasing Veccha into the wheel. Although no one speaks, there is an inaudible whisper. A command from the host.

"Go now," it says. "Do not return."

And Logan is floundering. Turning in circles. Tripping on the stones. Thoroughly confused by their presence. All the colour is washed from his face. He is looking now, searching for a way out. A path in the crowd. And when he can find no such thing, he starts out at a slow run. Stumbling awkwardly. Pushing past bodies. Falling and scrambling until he is through. And then he is sprinting. Leaping through the tall grass like a man possessed.

And everything is still, until slowly the Peigan break away. One by one. Turning cheerlessly in different directions. Scattering over the prairie like dandelion fluff. Until Wyoming is alone with Veccha. And although they do not speak—have no words for what the have witnessed—a message travels between them like brush fire.

Leaving Wyoming

AND SO WYOMING TELLS HER EVERYTHING. ABOUT THE MONEY. The murder. And the men from Pinkerton. They are sitting at the table in the cabin. Night is falling outside.

"We have to leave here," he says. And the word *we* parts the air like a moth. Beating and flapping its wings. Floating directionless.

"Where is the money?" she asks, accepting the presumption. And the moth flaps away to the rafters and is forgotten.

Wyoming reaches down beneath the table. With both hands he removes the oversized mule-ear boots. Worn leather scuffed a neutral grey. Still sporting their OK spurs. One after the other, he empties them onto the table. Notes of different denominations. Wrinkled and folded into balls. Sour and damp. Some of them torn. Others ruined completely.

"I used to stuff them with newsprint," he tells her by way of explanation. "I thought no one would look."

Veccha picks up the individual packages. Opening them one by one. Her small eyes do not blink.

"How much is there?"

"Almost thirty thousand dollars." His words fall like stones. "Less whatever's no good no more. And those I ruined myself."

Veccha looks up into his face.

"It's unsigned. Useless."

Her eyes drift up as she thinks.

"What were you planning to do?"

Weather can change on a whim on the prairie. Winds have been known to move frogs. Whole schools of fish. Horses have disappeared overnight. As they make plans into the darkness, lightning breaks open the sky and rains swell in from the south. Fall out of a bone-dry evening on the burnt earth of Alberta. The Assiniboine Territory.

Veccha heats the iron over the stove. Presses carefully into each bill. Restoring its shape. Cautious not to singe edges. Burn through the centre. Sometimes, she is not careful enough. It is late. Her arms are heavy with fatigue. But there is much left to do. Despite the wind and the unseasonal rains that drive into the cabin like nails, the room is as hot as a bellows. She is forced to remove her dress. Wyoming goes for a walk.

"Australia," she repeats to no one but herself. The childhood dream. Ayers Rock. She can still recall the details of Robert's descriptions. He was niggardly when it came to telling stories, but she couched her questions in the guise of scientific inquiry. Sifting his formal responses for signs of the truth. And there are his journals. Surely it too was a place of great power. Equal to Milk River. *Asinipai'pi.*

They will need travelling clothes, the appearance of means. At least until they can purchase something better in Vancouver. They will attach Logan's horse to the old cart for the trip to Lethbridge. From there, they will take the train over the Rockies. But first, she must concern herself with the money.

She works by oil lamp. Each note receives the same attention to detail. The fine cursive hand of her father. The hours of practise paid off. She hangs each finished forgery on a makeshift clothesline strung across the kitchen. All her energy is focussed upon this. Although there are other problems. Things not so easily fixed. Like a passport for Wyoming. His illegal entry into Canada. And underneath all this, the vision. The trial yet to come.

And so she works on into the hours before morning. Writing slowly and carefully. Outside the rain falls. With no end in sight.

Wyoming watches the river expand. It is churning now. No longer the placid pool it once was. The waters cut into the banks. Lift layers of mud and sod, which are carried downstream and eventually drowned. Small trees float past like dangerous fish. The sun is up. But hidden by clouds. Veccha is asleep finally. The money is finished. But still the rains come.

He is skittish now. Having lost the confidence he gained the day before. The rain is unsettling, a random force delaying their departure. He is pleased with Veccha's reaction. Her complicit aid. Her excitement over Australia. But somehow, he does not believe in happy endings. They have no plan to get him out of the country. The banknotes could be noticed as forgeries. Around him the rain falls in glistening sheets. And the waters rise.

On the third day of continuous rain, the river overwhelms the yard. The same stretch of fence that they replaced last week is carried downstream. Big trees. Full-grown cottonwoods and lodgepole pine rip through the river like half-drowned men-of-war. Crashing into each other and tearing out portions of earth from the bank. Refuse from the farms upstream near the Milk

River settlement jettisons through, navigating the dangerous currents.

A second arm branches off from the original river, wends its way through the yard behind the cabin. By nightfall the house is an island. They can hear the cow bawling in the barn. The horse snorting. By morning, the chickens are gone. The whole coop carried away in one piece like an arc.

Finally, on the evening of the fourth day, the rain abates. And the river collapses upon itself. Freeing the yard from its grasp. After days with no light, the moon rises over the cabin. Soft and white in the sky.

That night, after the rains have given way to clear skies, Veccha cannot sleep. Her mind is alive to the nightsong of frogs. Beside her, Wyoming slumbers dreamless, after days of nervous pacing in the close rooms of the cabin. Of planning impossible rescues of the cow. Everything is in place for their departure. But still there are variables. She knows that she should sleep. That there are still trials ahead. But there is an unconscious thrum in the back of her mind. A memory. A vision. The man she has been dreaming for days.

The fact of their leaving rushes over her now that all the preparations have been completed. Never again will she make the solemn trip to the coulee wall. And Two Bears. Already receding from her. Quick as the Milk River pulls away from her yard. The new boy beside her is still such a mystery. And in so many ways, he is not. And Robert. Poor Robert. His body in an African field. Returned to the earth as a stranger. She did believe that she loved him once. Perhaps she did.

Like all things, his passage could not have been random. It was he who saw her through the first leg of her journey. Set her on an intercepting path with the boy. Such a careful weaving.

And so as her mind winds down, she approaches the edges of sleep tentatively. Were it not for the one last sound before she goes under, she might be sleeping already. So this is it.

Wyoming's revolver hangs from the bedpost like a forgotten fruit. She does not hesitate. Already she has performed this act over and over in her dreams. Naked, she steps to the floor. Removes the cool metal gun from its holster. It has a sterile smell. The weight of it in her hand is the only surprise. She considers, for a moment, waking the boy. But there is no time. There never is.

She stands still by the window, obscured by the billowing sheer fabric she has herself fashioned. Her nipples harden in the cool breeze, and all her senses lean out, sending forth feelers into the room beyond the curtain. She is so certain. The vision. The memory. And then she hears it clearly this time. His entrance is an otherwise silent film. He is a large man, and the room seems impossibly small around him. She is not sure, but she thinks that she sees him smile. And then, as through some sort of sixth sense of his own, he raises his head like a sleepy bear.

Two round eyes. Black and lightless as coal. They exchange glances, and then he speaks. The word she can never make out in her dreams.

"Rose."

The gun in her hand belches black flame and smoke, but the bullet sails clear into the sod wall behind him. She is not prepared for the recoil, and it sends her crashing backward into the washstand. The real world begins where the dream ends.

Wyoming is out from under the covers before the man can process what has happened. He launches himself off the edge of the bed like a catapult cut clear. Striking the dark figure just above the belt. Veccha can hear the wind trounced from his diaphragm like the grunt of a pig. Both men land hard on the floor. The loose planks snap under the violence of their assault. The big man's gun is thrown clear of his reach.

Veccha loses them in the dark, and all she can hear is the sound of two forms struggling like mice in the ceiling. When she regains her feet, Wyoming's bare back is visible in the night. He is hunched over the body of the big man. The full force of his fists reigning down on the face beneath him. For a moment, she believes that Wyoming might subdue the intruder. That her dreams have misled her. But then there is a flash of light, and Wyoming feints away to avoid the blade of the knife.

Their roles are reversed now. The boy is eclipsed by the big man's cloak. Veccha can no longer see the knife. She levels the pistol again. Only a few feet away. She has been here before. It is as though some ancient drama is taking its course. And even though she has possessed her clairvoyance since birth, it is only in the last few days that she has come to understand what it is. Not the curse she always believed it to be. Not a gift, either. But a test. Like a game of chess you know that you have lost, but see through to the end for the sake of your dignity. Morality is part of it. Guilt. And happiness too.

And for the second and last time in her life, Veccha shoots another living being. This time, she does not miss.

The two sit in the straight-back chairs at either end of the table. The body lies on the floor where it fell, like a forgotten garment. For a while, nothing passes between them but silence. Dawn is still hours away. At one point, Veccha is tempted to rise and make tea—anything to make the time pass more quickly, change her thoughts—but somehow that seems sacrilegious.

Wyoming has the gun now. It dangles between his parted knees, hanging loosely from his left hand. He pried it gently from her unforgiving fingers. The smoke from its belching has dissipated, but the scent of gunpowder is still strong and pervasive. Veccha thinks that it will never leave these walls.

After what feels like an eternity, she manages, "Who is it?"

But Wyoming only shrugs.

"I never met him in my life."

Veccha looks across the table to where the boy is hunched like a sorrel nag.

"You have now."

Coming over a ridge on the Western Trail, just across the border from Nebraska on a late-season drive, Wyoming once spotted a lone grizzly. The world was sloping away into the gentle folds of a valley. Plum bushes and scrub on frost-covered grass. And beyond that, the hint of blue hills. Wisps of cloud, backlit by the rising sun. And further still, although Wyoming could not see them, the grey range of the Laramies stood a silent sentry. The point men, cold and tired in their woollies, were too wrapped up in the cattle to catch the shaggy beast descending from the distant stands of stunted pine, ambling hungry and intent. Its mottled head tossing in anticipation. The large mouth lolling, pink and distinct.

Wyoming was riding flank—the swing man no more than one hundred yards off—and descending the same slope in an almost parallel line. It was so cold he could see the bear's breath, chuffing in quick intervals about his head like smoke signals. Wyoming was so taken by the animal's primal majesty, its obvious supremacy in this setting, that he could not speak. He was close enough to hit the beast with a shot from his revolver—surely no more than a bee sting against that rough hide—but he could not bring himself to draw. The animal was starving, or perhaps it was simply dying of old age. Whatever the case, its pelt was bug-eaten and spotty, coming away in large tufts of rotted hair. It would not last the winter, he thought.

Wyoming squinted down the line of cattle now entering the folds, and was able to discern the white form of a yearling, newly branded, astray from the heard. The swing man, closer to the calf, was already riding out to corral it. Just then, the bear began to lope awkwardly sideways, helter skelter, in an uneven trajectory toward rider and calf. The flash of movement must have attracted the men riding drag at the rear of the herd, for the horseman closest to Wyoming called out. But the cowhand riding swing caught sight of the interloper at that same moment and sounded the alarm up the line, reining his horse in on instinct. Wyoming set out at a gallop to intercept the grizzly that was no more than thirty yards from its target now. He could hear hoof beats behind him on the hard ground. At least two drag men were also in pursuit. Even the point man had stopped and was screaming a warning up to the trail boss, who rode oblivious at the head of the herd.

None of the riders was carrying a rifle. They were too cumbersome and might get caught in the reins. Wyoming loosed his lariat as he drew alongside the bear. The swing man was doing the same. With a practised gesture, both men released their ropes. Wyoming's struck first. The honda snatched tight with a zip, and the bear's head snapped back against the force of his own inertia. Wyoming was almost pulled from the seat of his saddle. He let go of the reins and made a quick grab for the horn with his left hand. Inverted almost, and hanging over the withers of his horse, Wyoming watched the bear collapse. When he righted himself in the saddle, he saw that the swing man had managed to snare the right front paw. One of the riders on drag swooped in and performed the same trick with one of the rear legs. Three ropes held the panting mass.

The bear huffed and yodelled. Its great head craning on an almost hairless neck. A second drag man arrived, pistol drawn. The herd marched stupidly past into the valley. The drag man fired the first shot before Wyoming could say anything, and the bear called out in an almost human grunt. The two others drew their own pieces and opened up on the struggling animal. One of them yipped in delight as his cartridge crashed into the grizzly's cheek, stopping its howl in mid-note. Wyoming looked away to the hills and the shadowed peaks behind him, trying to block out the sound of the animal's suffering. He was still alive in spite of all his weakness, struggling to set himself free. But for all his aversion to the tactics of his compatriots, Wyoming did not loose the rope. He held fast until the wrangler appeared with a carbine from the chuck.

The presence of the executioner quelled the excitement. The wrangler raised the gun and stared down the long barrel at the bear, who had raised himself to a seated position, like a thrown rider shaking his head. Its glassy eyes tried to focus on the earth before it. But the wrangler was quick. The bear toppled backward from the force of the shot. His ruined face cradled in the grass.

Wyoming remembers that no one spoke in the first seconds after the bear's death. Its mad dash for sustenance. Dead now because its struggle for survival was at odds with the cowboys and their herd. A fated confrontation. The eternal conflict.

Wyoming would recall this scene many times in his lifetime as something more than death.

Wyoming carries Webb's body on the back of his horse. It was a struggle to lift him this far. But Veccha will not tolerate his burial in *Asinipai'pi*. Back at the cabin she is packing their bags. Once out on the open prairie, Wyoming dumps the load to the ground with some difficulty. With his eyes closed, it almost appears as though the man is resting. Wyoming does not know this man, except for a name. Harbours no rancour toward him. No malice. His killing was a matter of self-preservation. He does not fault Veccha.

"Mackenzie Webb," he says aloud. As good a name as any, he thinks. If Wyoming must have a new one, he is glad it is this. Veccha removed the man's papers before they were ruined by blood. They are the key to their safe departure.

Wyoming cuts into the earth with a spade. Tearing through root systems that have not been disturbed since the beginning of time. Once he is through, the digging is good. He has decided that it will be a proper burial. And so he labours away the better part of the morning.

When it comes time to lower the body, he wonders what life the man is leaving behind. But for some reason, it seems to him a lonely corpse. Like the body of Jim Winters. Nonetheless, he cannot help but wish for some modicum of ceremony as he turns the body into the pit. However, Wyoming has never been to a funeral. And he has not the slightest inclination about what is said at moments like this. So in the end he opts for silence. The cold whack of the shovel against earth.

There is only one trunk in the cart when it leaves. Rumbling and bucking slowly through the bunch grass of the prairie. Veccha abandons a lifetime of accumulation behind her. Pots and pans. Farming equipment. Robert's rock hammers and files. His research notes, burnt in the stove. The mirror over her wash-stand. She props open the door of the cabin like a running invitation. By nightfall, mice will be into the stores, burrowing warm bodies into the wall. Soon the dark soil of the prairie will pile itself in the kitchen. Cozy up to the stove and eventually over-whelm the table and chairs. The wood planks in the roof will be the first to go, a year from now. In the night. The sod walls of the hut will follow. But eventually everything will be returned to the earth as a gift.

Wyoming urges the horse north, slouched on the buckboard. Veccha sits stiff as stone to his right. She does not look back. But it is not for the memory of Lot that she keeps her eyes on the bald hills to the north. Not out of biblical piety. She is afraid of what she will see there. Robert with his hands open and pleading.

Sand in the floor of his mouth. Silting his pores. She refuses to watch as the prairie reclaims him. And so the wagon ride north into Lethbridge is a silent journey.

Had she bothered with one last glance, for the sake of her memory, she might have seen Two Bears wading hip-deep in grass. His brothers around him as always. Each of them so pale now, they are almost lost in the blue wash of sky. Victims to aerial perspective.

Acknowledgements

I would like to thank my father for Butch and Sundance, and my mother for the paper and the pen. Thanks also go to Nancy Keech and to Richard Carter, who read the earliest manuscripts and offered valuable insight. I thank Wayne Tefs, my editor at Turnstone, for his professionalism and unflinching honesty during the latter half of the journey, and I would like to make special mention of Jeff and Courtney Wood, who first took me riding. But the one person who deserves the lion's share of both my affection and appreciation is my wife Caroline—my first and last critic, my biggest fan.

Although I cannot list all the books and authors I consulted during the course of my research, I would like to acknowledge those who contributed most. I could not have written this novel without *The Outlaw Trail: A History of Butch Cassidy and His Wild Bunch* by Charles Kelly; *The West*, an eight-part PBS series by Ken Burns; *The Landscapes of Southern Alberta: A Regional Geomorphology* by Chester Beatty; *In Search of Ancient Alberta* by Barbara Huck and Doug Whiteway; and *Legends and Lore of the American Indians* edited by Terri Hardin. Stan Gibson and Jack Hayne also warrant thanks for their research on the little known Marias Massacre; and for their various articles and journal publications, I am grateful to Beth Gibson, Michael W. Johnson, Wayne Kindred, Jeffrey D. Nichols and W. Paul Reeve. Finally, both the Pinkerton Service Corporation and The Provincial Museum of Alberta merit my appreciation for their informative Web sites.